# Matched to The Pack

### Curvy Omegaverse Reverse Harem

## Layla Sparks

# Contents

# Things to Know...

**Omegaverse Terms**

A few things to know regarding the omegaverse world. The people in the omegaverse display a more canine or wolflike behavior. Some books involve shifting into wolves. This series will have minimal shifting. This story will not have shifting.

Here are some terms that will be helpful to know (*note: these definitions pertain to my stories):

**Omega**: A female or male who would often have multiple partners to help them during heats. Usually has a particular scent that alphas find very appealing and unable to resist.

**Beta**: Like a normal human, but in the wolf world

**Alpha**: Powerful and looked upon as the leader, and they gravitate to omegas. They also have a scent to attract omegas.

**Slick**: Secretion from the privates

**Heat**: A period where an omega needs to mate - akin to ovulating in human females.

**Knot**: When an alpha mates and omega, and the base of the penis swells, locking the alpha and omega in place.

**Rut**: Alphas can go into rut phase, similar to heat. Sometimes an omega's heat will bring it on.

**Scent blockers**: Can come in pills or as a cream. Blocks an omega scent from attracting alphas.

**Heat Suppressants**: Stops an omega from going into heat

# Content Guide

**If you don't have any triggers, please skip this page to avoid spoilers!**

**For any questions regarding triggers, please email: author_ laylasparks@yahoo.com**

- Double Penetration

- Menage

- Group Play

- Backdoor (anal) Play

- Kidnapping (forced/withholding pleasuring - chapter 26)

- Pregnancy

- Domestic Discipline/ Spanking

- Claiming bites

*For readers who prefer not to read about pregnancy or babies, please*

LAYLA SPARKS

*skip the bonus epilogue.*

# *Chapter 1*

### Jade

*Dear Director,*

    *I am writing to inform you of my decision to resign from the nurse position at Howl's Honor Hospital. I understand this is short notice, but I have decided to take a break from nursing. I cherish all the years working here, and thank you for the opportunity.*

*With all due respect,*

*Jade*

I was terrified and excited to hand in my notice as I read over and over until the letters blurred. I clutched the piece of paper between my fingers in the breakroom, straightening the crinkled edges.

"Hey, Jade, what do you have over there?"

I looked up at Keera as she sat across from me at the table. She was wearing blue scrubs today, always looking extra clean and neat. She was the doctor of the team I worked in and the only reason I stuck it out for so long. But now, I hated the thought of breaking the news to her that I was leaving the company.

We weren't just co-workers. We were best friends, and that made it harder.

"I don't know how to say it," I said, hesitantly looking down. I set the paper down on the table.

"Are you going to make me wait forever?" asked Keera, her eyes twinkling. "I'm probably not going to like what you're about to say next. Am I right?"

"You're right," I said in an even voice. "I'm about to quit this job. I'm going to give this notice to Lucia. Please don't be mad."

Her eyes widened, but she smiled. "I knew it. I feel sad about this, but I knew this was coming."

"What do you mean?" I asked, surprised.

"You weren't happy at your job, and I could feel it," said Keera. "And you always talked about the next party planning adventure or interior design. What do you plan on doing, though? Did you tell your family yet?"

I always took on odd gigs here or there, helping out with any party that would come up. And now I had a bigger gig helping my cousin with her wedding planning which I was stoked about. During my job as a nurse, constantly seeing pregnant omegas have babies with their alphas doting on them got tiring.

I didn't have a pack of alphas and had never been mated before. I longed for it, but it just never happened. If an alpha showed an inkling of interest in me, I'd mess up and say something clumsy. Especially at the Omega Ball every year without fail.

"My mom is all about omega education and getting an honorable job," I said. "I can't tell them yet. Not until I'm successful with what I'm doing."

"You will be."

6

"Well, I'm about to go to the bitch's office," I said, and Keera smiled. Lucia was the alpha director of the hospital, and she was tough. I don't think I ever saw her smile. "I'll talk to you later."

"Text me as soon as you do it," said Keera.

I cleared my throat as I stood in front of the director's door.

This was going to be my last day working here, but putting in my notice was going to be the tough part. I worked tooth and nail to get this job. To prove to everyone that omegas could be whatever they wanted. But I wasn't happy anymore. Sweat beaded down my back as I knocked on the door twice.

Second thoughts ran through my mind. Maybe this was a bad idea. I'd lose my stable income. I would be broke.

"Yes?"

I twisted the doorknob, stepping into Lucia's office. Her office was immaculate, with a picture of her blond family on her desk. Lucia tapped her red fingernails on her desk, her hair set into a strict ponytail. Her black blazer didn't have a speck of dirt as she leaned back in her chair, her lips thinned with annoyance.

She always looked annoyed, especially around us omegas.

I handed her my letter, and she took it with a huff.

"It's my notice," I said quietly, biting my lip. I could literally hear my mother in my head, sad and disappointed in me. "I feel like it's time for me to move on and do something new."

Lucia's eyes flashed as she looked at the letter.

"Today is your last day?"

7

"Yes."

"Couldn't handle the pressure, huh? This job is tough on single omegas looking to screw a few alphas," she said snidely.

*What the fuck? This bitch...*

Without saying another word, I turned and walked out of her office for the very last time.

And I didn't look back.

When I got home that day, I flipped on the living room light in the cramped apartment I lived in.

The drive home after work in my rusty old car was a relief. Self-doubt, excitement, and uncertainty filled me during the entire drive. I couldn't believe what I just did. I'd contemplated quitting it for years but hadn't gotten the guts to do it. It just wasn't my passion.

I dropped my keys onto the coffee table, flopping on the couch. Every bone in my body was tired from my overnight shift and odd hours. Even the purse I wore felt like a brick as I dropped it on the floor.

Sighing, I relaxed on the couch, gazing at my numerous paintings hanging on the walls. I spent time after work and on my off days painting in my spare room of the house. I'd then hang them all over my living room. Covering the wall entirely in art.

I didn't have many clients who'd come over to look at my paintings and buy them, but when I did- the pay was worth it.

Slowly getting up as my thighs ached, I started a cup of tea in the kitchen. The rent was due sometime next week, and I had no savings.

It was probably irresponsible of me to quit, but I did have a gig to help with wedding venue design for my cousin this Saturday. It should be enough to cover me for a while. While the tea kettle boiled, I walked around the apartment, closing the windows. It was chilly, and I was getting cold.

Three series of knocks sounded on my door.

I sighed.

I didn't feel like seeing anyone today. I just wanted to relax, cry, or mope around for a little before I could celebrate my new life. It just wasn't a good time right now.

"Who is it?" I said upon opening the door.

"It's me, sweetie," said my mother, walking into my apartment without a care in the world. Behind her, my three alpha fathers followed her inside.

*Great. An impromptu visit.*

"What are you doing here?" I asked.

"We thought we'd check in on you since you didn't reply to my text for two days," said my mom, Steph. She was dressed in her college professor uniform, wearing her black pencil skirt and blazer. She had straight black hair with streaks of gray in it, while I had very curly hair. She was considered a stunning beauty back in the day, with alpha packs fighting for her attention. I felt like a disappointment in her eyes, even though she never said it. My dads, Jon, Seth, and Rob, cherished my mother like crazy, each attending to her different needs in the pack. Jon was the oldest of my fathers, with short gray hair, and he was pouring the tea I made in the kitchen, oblivious to our conversation.

"I've been so busy," I said quickly, which was a half-lie. Mom had been texting me about the Omega Ball constantly. I didn't want to go to the Omega Ball this year. Every year I'd go and have high hopes, but no one was interested. I was on the chubbier side and twenty-eight, which made me ancient for omega standards and not as desirable.

"The ball is tomorrow, and I thought we could go all together as a family," said Mom, sitting carefully on the edge of my couch like it would contaminate her. My apartment was too artsy and messy for my mother's taste. Her house was always immaculate, with minimal design and not a stain in sight. She would always be annoyed when I pulled out my paintbrushes and canvases in her house, but now I was free to do that in my own home.

"But Mom," I sighed. "I was going to skip going this year. It doesn't make a difference, and alpha packs aren't interested in me. I'm still freaking single, and I'm just going to continue to live my life."

"Jade," she said, her face wrinkling as she tried to understand what I was saying. She didn't look happy at all. I couldn't imagine what she'd say if I told her I quit my job. There was no way in hell she'd let me live that down. "You can't skip going to the Omega Ball. You're an omega and should support anything that helps other omegas."

Omegas were rare in Howl's Edge Island; I've heard this conversation a million times from her.

I was sick of it.

I was sick of being different and trying to prove a point to alphas who didn't care. Omegas were deemed incapable of anything except producing alpha babies for a pack. That long-standing belief still carried on today, with betas getting way more freedom. I had to constantly slather on my scent blocker cream so I could pass for a beta in the streets. An omega was in danger of getting kidnapped and sold if caught. We had distinct smells and auras that alphas could detect a mile away. I always stayed my distance from a large hulking alpha for fear of getting taken into his pack or sent to the Omega Auctions.

"If anyone treats you badly at the Ball, we will handle them accordingly," said my father, Seth, who was balding and the tallest of the three.

He always advocated for me to follow my dreams even though it wasn't something my mom agreed with. Mom was the more practical one. When I was a teen, I'd go to him for everything that bothered me about school and the bullies I'd face back then. He held no judgment and quietly listened, comforting me when I cried. If anyone could convince me to go to the Omega Ball, it was him.

Crossing my arms, I leaned against the balcony door.

"That's right," said Rob, settling on the couch and groaning because of his back. He was big-boned and looked as large as Santa, especially with his full brown beard, speckled with white strands. His belly took a toll on his back, and I always had to massage his back during my childhood since my brother Jack would mysteriously disappear every time Rob requested it. "If any pack messes with you, Jadey, they're done for. We will keep a close eye on you. While Jon stuffs his face at the dance."

"What? I think you got that wrong," sputtered Jon, spilling tea on the front of his checkered shirt. Rob bellowed, holding his belly, and I laughed with them despite being annoyed by them barging in like this. My mom didn't even crack a smile. Instead, her eyes were hyper-focused on me – willing me to succeed and be the daughter of her dreams.

"Fine, Mom," I said. "I'll go to the Omega Ball tomorrow."

"Oh good," she said, the lines on her face visibly relaxing. "What's new with you, my dear?"

My heart stopped momentarily. I couldn't let her know that I had quit my job.

"Nothing much, just work," I said, gesturing to the green scrubs I was wearing. I looked away, not making eye contact as I spoke, hoping she wouldn't ask too many questions.

# Chapter 2

### Jade

"Your mom really wants you to mate up, huh?" said Vanessa.

My mom constantly glanced my way every few seconds while we stood off the dance floor in the ballroom. Her hawkish gaze was watching to see if any alpha would approach me.

"She does," I said.

For some reason, the alphas weren't approaching, and I wasn't wearing something ugly either. My dark purple floral dress hugged my breasts, showing off some cleavage, and it was honestly the best thing I had to wear today. Vanessa looked stunning in her silver dress that clung to her curves, her red lipstick accentuating her red hair. She was my brother's mate and had a pack of seven men.

Yep, *seven*.

While I had none. It sure was depressing as hell if I thought about it too much.

"I feel nervous about tonight," said Vanessa.

"Why?"

"I don't know. I'm a bundle of nerves for you. I have a good feeling

13

you'll find your mate."

"That's not happening," I said. "How're the children?"

"Lyra organized a little daycare here at the palace, so I dropped them off there," said Vanessa.

Lyra was the princess of Howl's Edge and also a close friend of ours now. I met Lyra through Vanessa. And I had met Tiana through Keera. We were a tight-knit group of ladies, and I would volunteer several times to help babysit for them. So it was nice that Lyra had someone from her palace handle it for tonight.

"I want to see Gabe and Lacy later," I said.

"Of course! They won't stop talking about you," said Vanessa with a smile. "They miss you."

At that moment, Alex came up to us, his eyes on his lady. A pang went through me as I longed to have that type of connection an omega had with her alphas.

"May I have this dance?" he asked, bowing his head and sweeping his hand with a flourish to Vanessa. I smiled when I saw Vanessa blushing, even after two years of being mated to her pack.

"Sure," she said, placing her hand in his, and he kissed the top of it dramatically. Then he looked over at me and shook his head apologetically.

"Sorry, I didn't say hi. Hey Jade, how are you?" he asked after ignoring my existence for an entire five minutes.

"I'm great, and yourself?"

"Doing great. Gabey and Lacey miss you," he said, sweeping an arm around Vanessa's waist.

"I know. Vanessa mentioned it. I can't wait to see them later," I said, noticing they were itching to get close from how they looked at each other, his hand around her waist. "Have fun dancing."

"Thanks," said Vanessa, looking at Alex with heart eyes.

I watched as they joined the other packs on the dance floor. They were either coupled up with omegas or meeting each other for the first time. My mother was near the drinks, talking to other moms and occasionally looking in my direction. I wanted to disappear so bad. Standing off to the side alone did *not* look good for an omega.

I might as well get auctioned off.

A tall, distinguished-looking alpha was approaching my way, and I tried not to make eye contact. But it was too late, and he was already standing before me, his hand outstretched with a smile on his face. He had straight gray hair, swooped back, revealing sharp brown eyes. A tinge of arousal went through me as I gazed at him. I never imagined I'd have a thing for older men, but here I was, swooning over this one.

"Would you like to dance?" he asked.

"Sure," I said. I could feel my mother's gaze on me, and I knew she was probably excited to see me accept a dance from an older alpha. He gripped my hand as he led me to the dance floor. His other hand draped my waist when the next song started.

"I'm Bruce. What's your name, may I ask?"

Gosh, he was so polite and soft-spoken. I didn't know what to think.

"Jade," I replied. His lips turned up in a smile.

"Beautiful name," he said.

His compliment made me blush like a schoolgirl, and I was easily perfuming now. My omega scent of apples was escaping the scent blockers that I rubbed all over my skin. It's been a while since an alpha held me so close. His scent of sandalwood and leather ignited

15

my senses as we twirled on the dance floor.

"Thank you," I said. "How old are you?"

*Damn it.*

I wanted to slap myself in the face after asking that question. It was so rude, and I just never seemed to have a filter.

"Forty-three," he said, his eyes twinkling. "Do you like older alphas, or do I scare you?"

"You don't scare me," I said. "Sorry about that rude question."

"Not many omegas are as blunt as you," said Bruce, chuckling. "It would take much more than that to hurt my feelings, beautiful."

"It's not often that I meet someone as charming as you," I said.

"You flatter me, but I have to say you have some good moves on you."

"I like dancing alone in my apartment," I said.

"I've been to a couple of these dances, but I don't think I've seen you before," he said, his hand pulling my waist closer to him as he dipped me.

"I come here every year," I said dryly.

He laughed out loud at my humor. Most people took it personally and didn't find me funny, so this was nice for a change. Someone that got me.

"I'm glad to have met you," he said when the song ended. "Would you like to grab a bite after the dance?"

I pulled away when the dance ended, surprised he still wanted to talk to me afterward.

"Maybe not tonight, but another time?" I suggested.

I liked him, but I never took things too fast like that. I needed time to lay in bed that night and daydream about him. I wanted to get hyped with the girls and tell them before I met up with him again.

He nodded eagerly. "Let me give you my number."

After exchanging phone numbers with Bruce, I decided to touch up my makeup in the bathroom. And also to escape my mother's curious gaze. Yep, she was definitely going to interrogate me. *Fuck my life.*

The hallway was large and elaborate as I walked down the regal purple and red carpeting, admiring the colors. The walls had paintings of past alpha kings of Howl's Edge. The deeper I walked down the massive hallway, the quieter it was from the mayhem at the ballroom. It was a welcome break, especially for me.

The bathroom was spacious, with ten stalls spread out from each other. A woman was in there washing her hands, leaving as soon as I entered. I set my clutch down on the counter and washed my hands as I stared at my reflection in the mirror. A few strands of hair came loose from my high bun, but otherwise, it still looked good.

I actually met an alpha today who liked me and took the time to talk to me. I wondered if he had a pack. Like a hot pack.

*Damn*, I should have asked him. But that would make me look desperate. Bruce was a pretty decent alpha, and I already enjoyed being around him.

Upon leaving the bathroom, I heard an obnoxious male talking loudly next to the door. Annoyed, I turned to look at him. He was an alpha wearing an immaculate black suit, glaring at his phone as he hung up. He looked towards me, and I quickly started to walk away. I didn't want his attention on me at all.

But that didn't work when he started calling out for me.

"Hey," he said. *Oh my God, what did he want?*

I stopped and turned to face him.

"What is it?" I asked rudely. He didn't need to shout at me and release whatever anger he had toward the person on the phone at me. He made his way over to me, staring at me up and down. He had shoulder-length messy black hair and stark emerald eyes. The unstable but handsome as fuck guys. *Just my type*, I thought sarcastically.

"You fit the requirements," he said, his eyes wide as he gazed at my cleavage. I took a step back, and he stepped towards me in the dark hallway.

I was so confused. *Was he out of his mind?* I was ready to scream if I had to. But no one would hear me over the noise of the ballroom.

"What requirements?" I asked, my voice coming out in a squeak.

He pulled out a card inside his suit jacket and handed it to me. It was pink and flowery with the words *Enchanted Nests* on the front.

"I run a dating agency for omegas to match with wealthy alphas," he said. His words were tumbling out in a rush from his excitement. "We made a match, but their omega ducked out at the last minute. I'm about to lose a great deal of money, and you fit their requirements."

"Listen, I'm not looking to get matched," I said.

"You're unmated," he said, cutting me off and sniffing the air for my scent. "It's free for omegas to join. Just think about it, okay?"

He nodded towards the card in my hand and walked away toward the back entrance. When he opened the double doors, a powerful gust of wind hit me, raising my dress around my knees, and I watched as he disappeared into the night. I shook my head as I tucked the little card into my clutch. I sure as hell was never going to call and get matched up to a random group of alphas.

*Did he think I was that desperate?*

But the little voice inside me begged me to take any offer.

18

# Chapter 3

### Jade

I didn't feel like getting out of bed the next morning.

My thighs and back ached after standing in heels all day at the Omega Ball. The heels I wore weren't a good choice, and this was the price I had to pay. Blearily opening my eyes, I noticed my blanket was off, and the top half of my body was freezing. Pulling the blanket up, I rolled onto my side and looked at my phone. It was ten a.m., and I could hear the rain pelting against my window.

I saw a text from Bruce and smiled.

**Good morning :)** - Bruce.

I didn't know whether to respond right away or not. He wasn't flaky, and it seemed like he felt a connection with me as well. So instead, I texted the group chat with Keera, Lyra, Vanessa, and Tiana.

**Ladiessss help** - me

**What is it?** - Keera

She was always the first to respond to me.

**I met an alpha last night, and he texted me this morning. Should I respond right away?!** - me

**Omg yes** – Vanessa – **What did he say??**

**But it's going to make me look desperate. He said good morning** – me

**You _are_ desperate, bitch lol** - Keera

**Text him back. Who is he?** - Vanessa

**An older alpha. Bruce. Refined and hot and everything**. - me

**Damn girl, u snagged a good one** - Tiana

Then another text came in. This time from my cousin, Shanna. Closing out the group chat, I opened the text, and my heart sank immediately.

**We have to cancel plans, Jade. I'm sorry. We're postponing the wedding :/** - Shanna

_Fuck._

There goes my rent money for this month. The emergency money I was relying on.

**No worries. Focus on you, okay?-** me

**Thank you, babes** - Shanna

Sitting up in bed, now wide awake and alert, I couldn't believe what just happened.

Now that my cousin's wedding was postponed or canceled, there was no way I could make the money I needed in two days for rent. As I opened the curtain in the living room, I looked out at the gloomy day. The rain was coming down hard. It was rare when it rained on Howl's Edge Island.

I couldn't ask my family for help.

They still thought I was working at _Howl's Honor Hospital_. And my brother was taking care of his omega, children, and his pack. I couldn't ask him for rent money. This was entirely my fault for relying on my random gigs for support.

I turned away from the window and noticed my glittering clutch abandoned on the coffee table where I had left it last night. Opening it, I saw a pink card and was suddenly reminded of the strange man in a suit from last night outside the bathroom.

Did they really match up omegas with wealthy alphas? *Have I stooped low enough for this?* And I already had a spot as a replacement for the runaway omega.

I decided maybe I *was* that desperate.

If I didn't like the alpha pack, I would ditch them. But I had no choice. I had no stable income and would have nowhere to live if I was kicked out. I couldn't imagine moving back in with my parents and answering my mom's overbearing questions about my job.

I wouldn't have the artistic freedom I wanted.

So I picked up my phone and dialed the number on the card.

"Hello, this is *Enchanted Nests*, where all your mating dreams come true. May I ask who's speaking, please?" said a chirpy female voice on the other end.

"This is Jade," I said. "I was just…"

She cut me off. "We were looking forward to your call. Do you have time to come in today for the interview?"

"Yes," I said, put off by her already.

"Great, we'll see you today at three. Do you have the address of our location?"

After sorting out the address and hanging up on her, I seriously doubted whether or not I should go through with this.

The drive to the dating agency was hellish.

The rain pelted furiously against my windshield, obscuring my vision of the road. Once I reached the agency, I was relieved to finally park the damn car. Grabbing my umbrella, I struggled to open it while standing in the rain and getting soaked. The space in my car was too small to unleash the umbrella inside of it.

The building was tall- made of glass, and looked professional. The words *Enchanted Nests Agency* on the front were embossed in gold. It wasn't some rinky-dink establishment. Suddenly, I felt self-conscious and not dressed for the occasion. I looked down at the raggedy jeans I was wearing with my black shirt with a picture of a rose in front. I looked like the poorest omega to ever step foot in here.

I ran across the parking lot and made it to the building, my shoes soaked through.

The door was tall, well above my height, swinging open automatically for me.

Walking inside, I took in the beige and gold tones of the walls and carpeting. Upon entering, there was a high desk made of marble and a blond beta female sitting behind the desk. Her hair came in waves around her shoulders, and she wore a dress with a name badge with *Chelsea* on it. She pursed her lips upon seeing me enter. I know *I* would be confused if I saw some chick wearing jeans entering an establishment like this.

*But whatever.*

She was going to have to get used to it.

"Hi, how may I help you today?"

"I'm here for an interview. I have an appointment today at one," I said.

"Your name?"

"Jade."

She typed endlessly on the computer with her long nails while I stood there, getting annoyed. She was the same girl on the phone, if I wasn't mistaken. If she didn't want me to be there, she could just say so. I didn't have much patience for bullshit, and I could sense it a mile away. When she was finally done making me wait, she looked up with a large smile.

Fuck that. This Chelsea bitch knew what she was doing.

"Third floor, and it'll be the room to the left. Room 204," she said.

"Kay, thanks," I said.

My wet sneakers squeaked on the shiny floors as I walked to the gold-covered elevator doors. In the elevator, I contemplated what the hell I was doing here. My heart was starting to beat faster, and my breaths were coming in short. I was way out of my element, but if I was going to get matched to a wealthy alpha pack, it would solve all my problems. When I saw my best friends with their packs, I was envious but also happy for them. Maybe this would be the only way I'd find my happily ever after.

I wanted to faint when the elevator reached the third floor. Regardless of how much I wanted a pack, I still wanted to run.

I could find another way to pay my rent.

This idea was so stupid.

*Breathe, Jade,* I told myself.

When I reached room 204, the door was already wide open.

It looked like a conference room with a long table with four alphas sitting behind it. A whole pack was about to interview me, and I was settling into full panic mode. The alpha I met outside the bathroom was there, dressed impeccably in a suit, and my heart nearly stopped when I saw someone else there.

Bruce was there, too, looking distinguished in his suit. And he looked just as surprised to see me.

# Chapter 4

### Jade

"Please sit," said the bathroom guy who had given me the dating agency card.

Swallowing nervously, I walked inside the conference room- feeling like this was a job interview instead of a dating agency where single omegas looked for love.

It wasn't very welcoming, and I could already see what needed to be done to re-design this room. Make it warm and welcoming for omegas. If they were going out of business, I wouldn't be surprised.

I clumsily pulled out a chair, blushing when it almost toppled over. The rain from my umbrella dripped loudly onto the marble floors in the quiet of the room. I tucked it between my feet under the chair hurriedly.

"The rain out there is pretty crazy," I said awkwardly. I was trying to break some of the tension in the room, and I didn't dare look in Bruce's direction. He probably understood why I didn't respond to his text this morning.

"It sure is. The rain's coming down hard," observed the bathroom guy, looking at me with a slight tilt of his head. He was pretty intimidating but hot as fuck when he wasn't rushing away from me in a hurry. "I'm Caleb."

Okay. So the bathroom guy had a name.

Caleb introduced the alpha with the short red hair next to him as Dravin, who was stocky, and the blond alpha with messy ringlets was Nick. Then there was Bruce.

I nodded as if I was meeting Bruce for the first time. Thank god he didn't say anything about meeting me yesterday.

He kept things professional, and I relaxed more in my chair.

"We will ask you a few questions to make sure you're a good match for the pack," said Nick. "Is that okay with you, Miss Jade?"

He was quickly writing down a few things on a piece of paper. He looked like he didn't like wasting time on small talk and worked quickly.

"Yes," I said.

"How old are you?" he asked, his gray eyes staring into mine. It was unnerving.

"Twenty-eight," I said. He didn't bat an eye as he wrote that down.

Bruce asked me the next question, and I was totally unprepared for it.

"Why are you here, Jade?"

He wasn't looking down at his papers or anything. He was fully focused on me, which made me even more nervous as I scrambled to gather my thoughts. All I could focus on was the stupid umbrella dripping all over my shoes and soaking my feet.

"I'm here to look for love," I said vaguely, looking down at the table, studying each fissure of the wooden material.

"Why haven't you found love?"

"I was very focused on my career, and before I knew it, I was getting older," I said.

"What do you work as?" asked Caleb, crossing his hands on the table.

"Nurse," I replied slowly. I wasn't sure if I should tell them the entire truth of it all. That I was broke and needed a wealthy alpha pack to save my ass. It was embarrassing but not something I was going to readily admit.

"I sense something is off with that answer," said Caleb. "I've been interviewing for years. Are you lying about something, omega?"

"I *am* a nurse, but I quit to pursue my real passion for art and design," I said. *Damn him*. He was smart and could detect a lie. Some alphas were like that, and not all were blundering tall macho men.

"So, unemployed?" asked Nick, writing furiously on his clipboard.

My stomach flipped. *Were they going to reject me now?*

"That's perfect," said Caleb. "Exactly what the Onyxpaw Pack are looking for. They are old-fashioned, looking for a nice homely omega. All we need to do now is get your measurements, and we can set up an official meeting with your future pack."

Oh no, I thought. *Did they want a compliant, unemployed omega?!* I wasn't sure if I wanted this after all.

"Measurements?"

"Beth should have been here by now to measure you," said Nick. "What's the holdup with Beth?"

Caleb picked up the phone from the desk and quickly spoke to someone.

"Beth called out today," said Caleb, his eyes flashing. Then he turned to me. "I will measure you myself then."

"What do you mean?" I asked again. *What was he measuring exactly?*

"The Onyxpaw Pack has a certain requirement regarding your body," he explained. "Please remove your shirt and jeans."

"Are you serious?" I asked, shocked. I already felt self-conscious about my body.

I was chubbier than the average omega.

"Without any measurements, unfortunately, we won't be able to continue with you," said Caleb, standing up with a measuring tape in his hands. He walked around the table, leaning against the edge while waiting for me.

I slowly stood up, extra aware of the alphas staring at me.

"Right here? In front of them?" I asked.

"Trust me, this is perfectly normal," said Caleb, his voice betraying impatience. "Omegas have to get measured. Now please remove your shirt and jeans."

*Was I wearing my good bra today?*

I hoped to the moons I wasn't wearing torn underwear either.

My hands shook as I lifted the hem of my shirt, revealing my stomach. I had never undressed in front of an alpha. Let alone a whole pack of them. I didn't dare look at their faces as I whipped my shirt off, letting it drop.

*Shit*, it fell on top of the wet umbrella.

I quickly picked it up and threw it on my chair. I looked down at my blue sports bra that I had put no thought into wearing. My face was so red by the time I pulled my jeans off, revealing my high-waisted cotton underwear, which covered my belly button.

Letting out a long breath, I watched as Caleb's eyes scanned my body from head to toe. His mouth quirked into a flash of a smile upon noticing my underwear.

*Great.* They all probably thought I was the most un-sexiest omega alive, and no wonder I was still single.

He wrapped the tape measure around my chest, his fingers pressing against my nipples as he tried to hold the tape measure steady. I tried to regulate my breathing since his closeness made my heart pump faster than a rocket.

He smelled fucking amazing.

I inhaled his alpha scent mixed with rich cologne. His watch sparkled at every angle as he tightened the tape measure around my breasts, calling out the numbers to the alphas as Nick wrote them down. My nipples hardened every time his fingers brushed past or tweaked them. Warmth curled in my belly, and my pussy was getting wetter each time he did that. For some reason, the glint in his eyes exposed the fact that he knew what he was doing. Toying with me without being able to claim me as his.

And if I said anything, it would make me look crazy.

So I kept quiet as he measured my waist next.

"Healthy hips to bear robust children," he said. "Time to measure your thighs next. Spread your legs for me, please."

When I spread my legs, his nostrils flared.

My apple scent was strong because of how much slick I was producing right now. I was wet as hell, and he knew it. I suddenly wondered if he hated my smell as he bent his head, wrapping the tape around my right thigh. I took a shower before getting here, so I couldn't smell that bad.

He quickly pulled away from me, like he couldn't get away fast enough. Like he was allergic to me, and I felt mildly hurt by that.

"Done?" I asked.

"Done," he said. "The receptionist will take a picture of you up-front, and then you are free to go. We'll call back to schedule an appointment with your matched pack if they approve."

It had only been five minutes of driving before I gave up and parked next to a children's playground. The rain was coming down hard, and it was dark now, making visibility impossible for me. My car was pretty ancient and tiny to go against mother nature right now.

So I sat in the car, hoping to wait it out, watching the swings fly wildly in the wind.

After the interview, I felt weirded out that four alphas had seen me uncovered. I couldn't even look at Bruce the entire time. Looking down at my phone, I didn't see any further texts from him either. He was probably disgusted after seeing me. I wasn't the magical belle he'd met last night at the ball.

This was me today. The *real* me. Whether he liked it or not.

Whatever. I'd soon get matched up to a wealthy pack and be free from all my problems. I couldn't wait. After all, I've met most of their requirements. So there shouldn't be a reason I'd get rejected unless my physical measurements put them off. And if it did, screw them.

Suddenly my phone went off with a loud beep.

A flash flood warning. *Nooo*.

"I have to get home," I muttered to myself as I started up the car again. I tried to back the car out, but the tires had sunk into the mud. "No, no, no."

I tried to move forward and back, but that only served to push the tires deeper into the mud.

I was fucking stuck out here, and there was no one around for miles.

# *Chapter 5*

### Caleb

"What do you think of the omega?" I asked my pack as I organized the notes in front of me.

"She's exactly what the Onyxpaw Pack is looking for," said Dravin gruffly, clearing his throat. "Attractive omega, that one."

"Voluptuous in all the right places," sighed Nick, rubbing his hand frustratingly through his hair. "Let's keep her for ourselves, boss."

"N...no," I said, hesitating for a moment.

She was attractive, yes. But she wasn't my type. I needed a submissive omega. One who would love to be taken care of at all times. To be carried, fed, and fucked constantly. Jade would find it creepy, and she was blunt.

Bruce was abnormally quiet.

Usually, as the oldest member of my pack, he relished giving input on the omegas that came into our office.

"What about you, Bruce? Should we tell the Onxypaw Pack the good news?" I asked, wondering what came over him.

He seemed lost in thought, his fingers intertwined on the desk.

"I didn't tell you all this, but I met her yesterday," Bruce finally admitted. "At the Omega Ball, we genuinely connected, and now she's here? None of this makes sense."

*Oh.* Fuck.

It was completely my fault that Jade was here. I was the one who gave her our business card and invited her here during the Ball. But I wasn't about to let Bruce know this. He shouldn't get attached to a client at all, or else the pressure to bring her into our pack would be enormous.

I wasn't going to deal with that pressure.

"Well, it looks like your connection didn't mean much to her," I said coldly. We needed to secure this million-dollar deal with the Onyxpaw Pack.

Bruce shook his head in disappointment. "I just can't believe she'd do that. Figures it was all in my head."

"So we agree to match her with the pack?" I pressed.

"Yes," said Dravin, his face glowing with excitement at the prospect of the money. We already ran a successful agency, but each deal was still exciting and fresh as the last. But as soon as I picked up my cell phone, it began to blare with a flood warning.

"Shit, the omega is out there driving," I said, my heart racing. I couldn't allow this omega to get into any danger.

She was important. A prized possession I couldn't lose.

"If she's smart, she'll stay sheltered someplace," said Dravin. "Call her."

I dialed her number, and the phone went straight to voicemail.

"She's not answering," I said, getting up and pacing around as I stared out the vast windows. The rain was coming down hard, and

I could see the beginnings of a disaster on the ground. A couple of inches of rain, that was quickly piling up.

"Hey, Jade," said Bruce.

Somehow he had gotten through to her on the phone. Racing to his chair, I ripped his phone out of his hands. I can't believe she had the nerve to ignore *my* call.

"Hey Bruce," she was saying.

"Jade, it's me- Caleb," I said urgently. "Are you driving right now?"

She was breathing quietly on the other line.

"I am," she said. The background noise of the rain pelting on her car sounded ominous.

"How far away are you from home?"

"Not far," she said vaguely, but I could sense the dishonesty in her voice. "Tell me the truth omega."

"You sound panicked for my life," she giggled, and I nearly threw the phone against the wall.

"I'm going to stay on the line until you get home," I said firmly.

"Fine, I'm stuck," she said. "My tires are stuck in the mud."

"Tell me *exactly* where you are, Jade."

### Jade

I sighed as I hung up.

Looks like I couldn't just sit here and wait for the rain to stop. Caleb would be here soon, barging his alpha self into my life.

That's how alphas were.

They felt the need to always be the hero and were super overprotective. I was used to taking care of myself and doing my own thing. My mother taught me to be strong, and the thought of being helpless as I sat in my car bothered me.

Leaning back against my seat, I closed my eyes and listened to the rain furiously pelting against my car. It was soothing, but I was freezing as I hugged myself. I had to turn off the engine in my car since my gas tank was less than half full.

I didn't realize I had fallen asleep until I woke up to a loud rapping at the passenger door. My heart was racing as my eyes snapped open, and I could make out the blurry figure of Caleb peering through the window at me. The gold iris of his eye glowed in the dark.

Damn, it was past sunset already.

I unlocked the door, and he got inside next to me. He made the car seem tiny with his muscular frame. His scent wafted around the car, intoxicating and alluring to my inner omega. His scent made me want to crawl all over him, to stick my nose in his neck and absorb him.

"Your tires look bad," he said abruptly, distracting me from my naughty thoughts of him.

"Yeah...I know."

"There's no way we can free your car today," he said. "But you can come with us to our place, and we'll return when the weather's better."

"Oh no, that's unnecessary," I protested, knowing where this was headed. From how determined he was to get here, I knew this was a losing battle. He would take me home with him regardless. "I can sit here and wait it out."

"Then I'll sit here with you," he said, reclining the chair back and crossing his arms over his chest. He meant it as he sat there. My mind raced with possibilities of how I could kick him out of my car.

"I can take care of myself," I said. He looked at me lazily, his eyes half-closed as he prepared to settle in with me.

"Not taking that chance," he chuckled. "You are worth a lot of money to me right now."

"Is that what I am?" I said indignantly. "A wad of cash to you?"

"No, of course not," he laughed. "You're funny, Ms. Jade."

*What an arrogant dick...*

"You can take your ass back to your giant truck over there before the flood gets worse," I said. "I'm fine right here, and I don't need you in here to keep me company."

"Doesn't a warm bed sound nice to you?" he asked, looking at my wet shirt and the goosebumps on my arm.

He traced my arm with a warm finger, and I shivered.

His touch held a depth of alpha energy and power that I longed to be enveloped in. My breathing quickened, and I knew I didn't stand a chance.

"It *does* sound nice," I said, my voice softening against my will. My inner omega was happy to be given this type of attention. The attention I longed for but didn't dare indulge in.

"Perfect. We will keep you safe and sound for your intended pack."

As I stepped outside the car, I wasn't prepared for the onslaught of rain.

My hair was plastered to my head by the time I reached his truck. Someone opened the back door for me as I ran up to it, and I saw his entire pack sitting inside. They quickly scooted over to make room for me as I sat there with my dripping hair and clothes squished between the door and Dravin. The warmth of the heater was like a warm blanket, and it felt so good. I sat across from Bruce, and for some reason, he didn't look pleased to see me there. Nick was sitting on the other side of Dravin.

Caleb began driving the truck as we all looked at each other.

"You must be freezing," said Dravin, removing his jacket and draping it over me. His body warmth still clung to the jacket, and I basked in the warmth.

"The jacket will get wet," I said, self-conscious.

"It's better than a sick omega," he winked. "We will take care of you to the max. Until you're sick of it."

I smiled, not sure to what extent he meant.

"She says she can take care of herself," said Caleb chuckling, and I pursed my lips with annoyance.

"What? So you don't think it's possible?" I asked, ripping the jacket off of me and throwing it back at Dravin. His eyes widened in shock at my behavior.

"Calm down. I'm only teasing," said Caleb. "Put that jacket back on."

"I don't need it," I said, rubbing my very-cold arms. I couldn't let him think I needed them. Not in the slightest. Especially when he was being such a douche about it. Dravin leaned closer to me, his short red hair brushing against my shoulder.

"Caleb loves to tease omegas because he can't get any of his own," he whispered, and I couldn't help but smile.

"I can hear you, jackass," said Caleb as Dravin gently set the jacket around my shoulders.

Once in a while, I'd glance up at Bruce, but his eyes were focused on the window- away from me. He didn't seem to want to talk to me at all.

*Was he that pissed at me*? We barely even knew each other, and it's not like I committed anything to him.

He had to get over it.

"Hi, Bruce," I said. Then teasingly. "Prepared to have me sleep over at your place?"

He lifted his eyebrows as his gaze turned towards me. My pulse raced with apprehension.

"Of course," he said mechanically. "We will try to make your stay as comfortable as possible." Then he looked away, and my heart sank a little. I didn't particularly appreciate that he wasn't his normal friendly self with me anymore.

It felt cold in a way. And it made me feel alone.

The ride was smooth with the truck, even though it got scary at times when the water was too deep. I couldn't believe I was about to stay out here all night. It looked impossible to get back home.

"Here we are," said Nick, peering out the foggy window. "Home sweet home."

# Chapter 6

**Jade**

My purse nearly fell into the harsh waters below when I stepped out of the truck.

Caleb appeared out of nowhere in front of the door. His arms outstretched as if to carry me.

"I can walk," I said. His black hair was soaked as he stood under the rain waiting patiently for me as if I was a petulant child.

"Jade, please," he said.

He was being overprotective again.

I sighed and allowed him to carry me. I could smell his earthy smell of wildness and musk as he carried me. The rain trickled down my face, and I licked it off my lips. I flinched in his arms each time the thunder boomed, but he held me even closer to him.

As he jogged through the flood waters with his powerful legs, I looked at the elegant architectural lines of his house, with its three stories and curved bays. Then, I looked over to the guesthouse outside of it. The windows were all boarded up except for a few, and the walls were singed with black blotches or fire.

"Looks creepy," I said out loud. Then I realized how rude it sounded.

"My mother lives there," he grunted, wading against the current of the water. His chest muscles were tense as he held me tighter against him, shielding me from the rain. "Don't worry, omega. We'll be inside warm and toasty soon."

The wind was biting against my skin, but we were inside the house before I could feel the full effect. He set me down on my feet and disappeared off into the dark house, flipping on the light switches. I hung Dravin's jacket behind the door and painstakingly peeled off my wet shoes and socks.

"There he is," Nick chuckled when Caleb returned, holding a towel in his hands.

"I have a bath running for you," said Caleb. "Please strip off your clothes."

I reached out for the towel. "I can wash myself, thank you very much."

"I wish to bathe you whether you like it or not," insisted Caleb.

"It's best to listen to him," Dravin muttered in my ear. "He has literal OCD about this. Caleb takes care of his omegas."

*What the hell?!*

"You want me to strip here? In front of you?" I said. I stepped back towards the door. "I'm not your omega, Caleb."

He shut his eyes in frustration, taking a deep breath.

"I'm not going to do anything to you. Except to take care of you and make sure you don't end up with a cold," he said. "Jade?"

He looked at me questioningly. Even if I ran out of the front door, I had nowhere to go. I would die out there.

It was either that or allowing an alpha to take care of me to the fullest. My chest was rising and falling in rapid breaths. I felt like I was suffocating. I should never have gotten out of my car.

"It's okay, take a couple deep breaths," said Bruce, sensing my panic and need for space. He rubbed my back in comforting circular motions. He brought his lips to my neck, and I felt his warm breath as he gently purred into me. His alpha vibrations were calming to me, easing me into normal breathing. "He just wants to take care of you."

"Get the bath ready, Nick."

I melted back against Bruce's frame. I could feel his wide, muscular chest despite the suit he was wearing. His hands swept around me, lifting my shirt by the hem. I allowed him to lift my shirt over my head. After all, they'd seen me half-naked at the agency today. But this felt way more intimate and less professional. Caleb watched as Bruce unsnapped my blue bra, but I still held it to my breasts in a panic.

"Don't be nervous," said Nick gently, tugging the bra from my hands. My face heated as I relinquished the bra, watching it dangle from Bruce's pale, hairy wrist. My breasts were exposed now, my nipples hard from the cold.

I sneezed.

"Hurry, we need to get her into the tub immediately," said Caleb. I could feel his gaze burning into my boobs as I bent down, pulling off my jeans. Then, hesitantly, I pulled my cotton underwear down my thick thighs while trying to cover myself with my other hand. It had been a while since I shaved, and I felt embarrassed as I kept my hand over it.

Who would have ever guessed that four alphas would be checking out my naked body tonight? If anyone had told me this would happen,

I would never have believed them. This was stuff an omega would dream about before getting officially marked and mated by her pack.

Caleb grasped my other hand and walked me toward the bathroom. The living room didn't have much, just vases of plants in every corner. This house looked lived-in, with the crumpled leather couch and the TV area surrounded by dirty plates. It was a medium-sized house that needed a little bit of help. An omega's touch would help.

When Bruce opened the bathroom door, I gasped.

The bathroom was spacious, adorned with marble flooring and walls. In the center of the room, the bathtub was a work of art carved from white marble with gold-plated faucets. It was full of soapy water, and the air swirled with the smell of essential oils.

"It's ready," said Nick, waving to the tub with a flourish of his hand.

I stepped into the tub, and it was pure heaven. My legs began to warm up to my knees, and I quickly sank my entire body into the tub, leaning inside until the water reached my chin. The warmth of the water soaked through my chilled body. The sound of thunder ripped through the night sky outside, and I could see lightning flash through the window.

"I'm so glad I'm not out there," I said, basking in the warmth. "Thank you so much, guys."

"No problem," said Caleb, who had grabbed a rag from the shelf.

"Wait, what are you doing? I'm in here now. I can wash myself."

"I'm going to wash you," said Caleb, wrapping one arm around my body to hold me still. "Just relax, omega. Close your eyes, and let us take care of you."

I was tired of fighting him. He would get his way no matter what, and frankly, it was less work for me. I felt highly spoiled as his strong hands massaged my shoulders with the soapy rag.

"I'll wash her hair," said Nick, and I felt a squirt of cold shampoo on my head. His hands felt divine as he carefully massaged my head until my hair was covered in bubbles and shampoo. My eyes began to close as I relaxed against the tub as Nick knelt behind me, washing my hair. Caleb's hands moved from my shoulders to my front. My chest rose and fell in anticipation as he swirled the rag around my left boob. His bare fingers would brush against my nipple, and I was getting aroused.

Thank goodness it was under the water, and they couldn't tell if I was horny. It was always obvious when an omega was aroused. They would be able to tell from my scent rising and the slick of moisture from between my legs. The water helped disguise it immensely.

"Bruce, get her something comfortable to wear and set it on my bed," said Caleb.

"We don't have any female clothing."

"Anyone's clean shirt will do."

I was so focused on Caleb's hands washing my belly and Nick massaging my head that I didn't care what he was saying. Next, Caleb was washing my legs and my thighs. I wasn't too self-conscious when he couldn't see any part of my body under the soapy water. His wet black hair hung at his shoulders as he concentrated on washing all around my thighs. I wanted to laugh since he was probably not used to larger thighs like mine. But I kept my eyes closed and nestled further into the water. I was getting used to alphas touching me now, and their strong hands felt so good.

His hand slid up my thigh, cupping my pussy.

My eyes flew open.

"Listen, I'm not your omega," I started softly. I calmly placed my hand over his. His eyes flashed as he gazed at my thighs peeking out of the water, his hand between them. My heart was beating fast as he gently squeezed my pussy.

"I'm simply washing you. Every part of you," he said. "I'm not going to suddenly knot inside you right here on the tile floor."

"Just hurry," I said, releasing his hand. When this alpha made up his mind, he was stubborn as hell.

I suddenly felt bad for his future omega. She wouldn't stand a chance.

His fingers circled my folds, stimulating me with every touch. I had to keep it together. I took deep breaths to avoid having an orgasm while he was washing my pussy. His pointer finger swirled around my clit, while his thumb massaged my pubic hair.

"Very hairy," he muttered, and my face turned hot. "Let me grab the shaver."

"No!" I moaned. It was so humiliating to be shaved. I sat there shaking in the tub, closing my eyes in frustration.

Caleb pulled a cabinet open, going through the shavers.

"It's okay, Jade," said Nick comfortingly. "Just pretend you're getting a wax...from a hulking alpha male."

"Not funny," I groaned as Nick began rinsing my hair.

"Stand," said Caleb.

If I stood up, I would be totally exposed. He'd see every part of me, and he wasn't even my alpha. But the command in his voice compelled me to obey, and I knew arguing would make things worse. Biting my lip, I stood up as the water dripped off my body. His eyes raked my body from head to toe without shame, lingering on the dark patch between my legs. I couldn't help but cover myself with my hand.

He swiftly pulled my hand away and began inspecting the hairs with his fingers. His thumb traced in circles around my pubic hair. My scent was getting deeper and covering the bathroom air the more I was aroused. The more he played with my pubic hairs, the more I freaked out inside, and then I began to feel the familiar warmth between my legs.

Slick began seeping from my core.

# Chapter 7

**Caleb**

T his omega was incredibly beautiful.

Water dripped from her thick dark eyelashes, her dark nipples, and her shapely thighs. I hoped the Onyxpaw Pack would worship every part of her. Even though she wasn't my omega, she would still be taken care of.

And I would make sure of that.

Nick grabbed handfuls of water, keeping her warm as I knelt in front of the omega, ready to shave her. She was trembling before me, aroused and ready for me despite her protests. She wanted me to do this. To take care of her.

I dipped the shaver in the bath water, soaking it before sliding it vertically over her pussy. With every stroke, her thighs trembled, and her scent thickened.

I brought a handful of water, rinsing her. The hair slid away, revealing her beautiful tiny pussy underneath. My cock was stiff as I rinsed her pussy and continued to shave her. She was shy, with her thighs closed tight.

"I can smell your arousal," I said. "Shutting your legs like that isn't going to help, little omega. I need to shave you thoroughly. Please spread your legs."

She huffed and spread her thighs an inch apart. I wanted to smile, but I didn't want to show her any weakness on my part. I had to be stern with her. She was the most stubborn omega I've ever met. I knelt closer to her until I could smell the whiff of her apple-scented pussy. My mouth watered, and I imagined savagely pounding into her with my dick.

But I couldn't afford the luxury of keeping an omega. She would bring in the big bucks to my business.

Plus, I was done with omegas after what happened to my pack wife years ago.

"Is this good?" she asked.

I could barely get a hand in between her legs. "Wider, please."

When she spread her legs to my liking, I gazed at her pussy folds lined with hair. Carefully, I shaved both sides while also noticing her engorged clitoris. This entire shaving session aroused her. I longed to tickle her clit, and give her the relief she wanted, but she needed to wait for her intended pack. They would take care of her sexual needs. If I sexually satisfied her, she would have no need to be with the Onyxpaw Pack. It was better she stayed aroused until we had lunch tomorrow with the Onyxpaw Pack.

As I rinsed her pussy, her clitoris felt heated and swollen. I rubbed around it but not directly on her bud. She let out an audible whimper but didn't dare say what was on her mind. She was too stubborn and too proud.

And that was good. It helped me not get too attached.

If she begged me to make her orgasm, I would immediately dive in, licking and sucking her pussy like no tomorrow. I wouldn't have a chance against her. She thought I was in control, but if she knew an omega's power over an alpha...

I continued to shave her pussy, ignoring her little sounds. Each tiny whimper or moan from her lips made my cock harder. I couldn't think straight with the warmth of her skin on mine, the hot tub, and the foggy air.

Her glistening little hairs soon disappeared. Her pussy was all clean now. I was proud of my handiwork as I ran my thumb along her clear skin. Nick had grabbed the towel, preparing to wrap her in it – to my dismay.

"Good job," he said to her.

"Wait, Nick," I said. "We're not done. Omega, please kneel and turn around. I need to wash your behind."

"What?!" she squeaked.

"Oh yeah, we forgot to wash her ass," said Nick. "The most important part."

"I have a name, you know," she said.

Jade's face flushed a deeper pink as she knelt in the tub, turning her back to me. I watched the top of her pale cheeks crown the water. I grabbed the rag and washed her bottom, starting with one cheek at a time, her butt jiggling in my hands as I washed her.

Nice and juicy.

I let the rag float in the tub as I reached between her cheeks, pressing my fingers up and down her crack. She gasped as she felt my bare fingers washing her little asshole. I spread her ass cheeks apart and watched her anus blinking, trying to shut me out. I poured a handful of water over it, rubbing her asshole around and around. She jerked like she was about to orgasm, and I quickly stopped.

"Now, we're done," I said, releasing her bottom. She stayed kneeling like that for an additional thirty seconds, hoping for more, but when it wasn't coming, she quickly scrambled up, blushing and confused.

"Um, that's all?" she asked, her voice hoarse.

"Yes, you did amazing," I said, not covering my apparent hard-on as she gazed between my legs, her eyes wide.

Nick wrapped her in the towel, and I helped her out of the tub. If she slipped and fell, I would never forgive myself. Her body was warm and soft after her bath. It felt amazing to hold her like this, only wrapped in a towel. She felt so vulnerable in my grasp.

"I'm going to take a shower," said Nick, and I nodded.

I led her by the hand to my room and was glad to see that Bruce had prepared a clean shirt for her which was lying in the middle of my bed.

"I'm going to grab the lotion," I said, leaving her in the middle of the room as I rummaged in my dresser. I pulled out a bottle of lotion and saw her lips twitch as I held it in my hands.

"And you're going to be the one to put it on me?" she asked.

She was learning quickly.

*Good.*

At least I'd have her trained for the next pack, and they would have to pay me extra money.

"Yes, lay on the bed, omega," I said. I knew she had a name, but she would get attached to me if I used it. It was best to keep emotionally detached from an omega that wasn't my own.

She carefully set the towel on the bed and laid on top of it. Her breasts were luscious, her nipples hard. Her pussy was pink and shaved nicely. I squeezed the lotion on my hands and got to work, starting with her arms and massaging every inch of her until she was yawning. When I got to her breasts, my cock danced as I squeezed each her breasts with the lotion, making her nipples stand out further. She was breathing hard, her breasts heaving up and down as I rubbed her nipples. Her skin was smooth and soft under my rough hands, and I loved the feeling.

It had been years since I last touched an omega like this. Ever since my wife...but I couldn't go there right now. I needed to concentrate on the here and now.

"Oh my god, I forgot," she said.

"What did you forget?"

"I don't have my scent blockers or heat suppressants," she said, worried.

"There's a high likelihood you won't go into heat tonight," I said, smiling. "It takes a while for that to happen. As for the scent blockers-if we can't handle your scent and want to rut you, we can keep you locked up in a room until it's safe."

"Okay," she sighed, closing her eyes. I felt an innate sense of alpha power as I watched her trust in me. It filled my basic primal desire to have my omega trust everything I said and give her body to me simultaneously. It wasn't something I took lightly at all.

*But she wasn't mine.*

Her scent was intoxicating as I rubbed the lotion around her thighs. Her skin would turn temporarily pink with every indentation of my fingers. I had to hold myself back from digging between her legs with my thick tongue. I wanted to devour her tight pussy. To lick her until she shouted my name over and over. This was temptation to the finest as I rubbed her feet next, my eyes glued to her pussy. Her eyes were still closed as she enjoyed the massage.

"I know you're tired," I said. "But do you want dinner? Dravin and Bruce are probably whipping something up."

"I just want to sleep," she said, yawning and sitting up. She grabbed the overly large shirt and draped it over her. The omega looked adorable in the gigantic shirt with no underwear. "Should I sleep on the couch?"

"No, you can stay on my bed," I said. "We only have four rooms in this house, so you can stay here."

"Are you sure?" she asked, yawning again, her eyes half-closed as she crawled to the pillow. I picked the towel up and smiled as I watched her snoring soundly fast asleep after her bath.

I hung the towel on a rack and went back over to her.

As I sat on the bed, I was uncomfortable as fuck with my raging hard-on. The omega was lying on her back, and I could see the hint of her pussy peeking between her legs. I watched her sleep for a half hour, watching as she adjusted herself. Her legs had spread on their own accord, and I watched her glistening pussy under the light of the lamp. Then, taking off my wet pants, I grasped my hard cock and stroked myself.

I squeezed the head of my cock, feeling pre-cum leaking as I gazed at her open pussy. Her legs were so beautiful, leading up into her perfect little pussy. I grasped my cock, rubbing harder, moving my hand up and down as I imagined sinking into her tiny hole. I imagined opening her up until she moaned uncontrollably. Fucking her tight cunt until her slick ran down her legs. To see her big breasts wobble up and down while her belly was round with my child. While Dravin takes her tight asshole, stretching her until she screams. Then finally, I would knot deep inside her, impregnating her again with my seed. And not allowing a drop to spill out of her pussy. To make sure she was pregnant at the end of her heat cycle.

*Fuck.*

I groaned out loud as my eyes rolled back in my head.

I looked down, realizing I spurted cum all over my pants on the floor. Breathing hard, I looked back at her sleeping form and quickly grabbed the sheets to cover her body. Any more temptation, and I would need to make her mine. I decided to sleep on the couch.

I wasn't taking any chances tonight.

# Chapter 8

### Jade

"Wake up, little omega," said a male voice behind me.

I groaned, burying my face in the pillow. It sounded like the alpha with the curly blond hair. Nick or something was his name. Recollection of the previous night made me squirm. They had all seen me naked last night. The pillow smelled like Caleb, as I inhaled his scent.

Caleb had shaved me last night. My pussy twitched at the memory. *Oh my god*.

"I'm still tired," I said, my voice muffled in the pillow. It was way too embarrassing to show my face to the alphas. And the bed was so warm, but I needed to pee.

"We have a big day today," said Nick, gently shaking my shoulder. "Today is your lunch with your matched alpha pack. And you need to dress up and look stunning."

"Wait, I thought you were taking me home today. What lunch?"

"We decided to have the Onyxpaw Pack meet you here instead of at the headquarters," said Nick. "No one wants to be out there stuck in the rain."

Groaning, I turned around, facing Nick who was lying next to me. His hands were crossed over his waist with one knee up. He wore dark jeans, a navy blue checkered shirt, a thin silver chain around his neck, and a small diamond earring on his left ear. His blond curls were tamed into a ponytail, and I had to admit he looked really good. I hoped the pack they had for me looked half as hot.

"I have nothing to wear," I said, tugging on my oversized shirt.

"Oh crap, you're right," he said. He glanced towards the window. "We can attempt to go shopping."

"Isn't it raining outside?"

"It slowed down enough, and our truck is invincible."

"Where's everyone?" I asked, sitting up.

"Bruce will join us for our shopping trip. Caleb is talking to someone to get your car towed," said Nick. "Dravin is on-duty to prepare the house for your big alpha meeting. Are you excited to meet the new pack we matched you with?"

"Well, they're not my pack *yet*," I said. "Normally, how does the process go?"

"We interview the alpha pack and the omega separately to make sure they're not crazy or anything," said Nick. "Then they meet. After the meeting, they tell us if they'd like to continue to see each other."

"So I'll have a choice to refuse if I wanted to?"

"Of course! It's a dating agency," laughed Nick. "Not the fucking Omega Auction."

For some reason, I couldn't fathom having a choice of picking which pack I wanted. To just pick and choose- not based on each other's scents. An alpha's scent may appeal to me, but he could be the biggest alpha-hole. Natural biology played a part in the survival of the werewolf blood in our veins on Howl's Edge. Excitement swirled in my belly at the thought of meeting them.

I couldn't wait to meet the Onyxpaw Pack and hoped to moons they were at least decent guys.

It was around eleven a.m. when we arrived at the Moon Cloud Mall, the biggest mall on Howl's Edge. It wasn't too crowded for a Friday, but it still had its fair share of betas, omegas, alphas, and an occasion delta security guard roaming around.

"Let's go to that dress shop over there," I said, pointing to the shop across from us. There were several dress shops, but one was for curvier ladies like myself. I loved coming here to shop whenever I wasn't working. I wasn't exactly great with money and it was something I needed to work on.

"Alright," said Bruce, quietly walking ahead of me for protection as Nick walked beside me.

Since I had no scent blockers, alphas would constantly look my way. Omegas were conditioned to hide their natural scent and allure since birth. I knew it was for my own protection. But if it meant alphas would start paying attention to me, I didn't want scent blockers anymore. Scent blockers were a thing to control omegas. A single omega could start a war between packs if they desired her, and it was also a way for the government to keep things under control. Beta females constantly envied us, even though we couldn't be our real selves. At this moment, I wasn't used to alphas gazing at me with a need and desire in their eyes.

In a couple hours, I'd meet my matched pack for lunch. My heart jumped again at the prospect.

*Would they like me? Was I finally going to have good news to tell my mother?*

As I scanned the rack for dresses, I was looking for a dress that would complement my figure. Nothing too formfitting or baggy. Three other people were in the shop beside the cashier, who was chewing on bubble gum, looking bored as she gazed at us like we were going to steal something.

Bruce had wandered off to the wall, looking at baseball caps.

"How about this one?" Nick asked me, holding out a sky-blue dress that had short fluttery sleeves. It looked fitted and flared out at the waist with a slim brown belt.

"Oh wow, it's so cute," I said, then looked at the price tag. "Maybe we can get something like it, but cheaper."

"Listen, it's on us," said Nick, his gray eyes darkening like a thunderstorm, and my stomach flipped. "Grab as many things as you need. You don't need to pay us back. This is your future, and you have to look your best."

"Thank you," I said softly.

"Also, we won't get paid if you look hideous," he joked, and I rolled my eyes.

"Alright then, where's the fitting room?"

I located the tiny fitting room hidden in the back.

The cashier didn't look too happy as she saw me entering the fitting room without talking to her. Nick and Bruce waited outside as I pulled off my shirt from yesterday, which had dried from the rain, and my jeans. When I slipped the dress over my head, the soft fabric glided against my skin. I took a deep breath and looked at myself in the full-length mirror. The vivid blue of the dress complemented my skin perfectly, and the fitted bodice hugged my curves in all the right places. The skirt flared out playfully as I twirled in the mirror. I couldn't help but smile at how fun and flirty it looked. Tightening the belt around my waist, created an hourglass shape and modern feel.

"May we see it?" asked Nick.

"Yeah, one sec," I said, twirling one more time in the mirror and then opening the door. Nick's eyes widened as he gasped. Bruce looked me up and down approvingly.

"You look like wife material," said Nick, grasping me by the shoulders and spinning me around.

"It might be a little too sexy," said Bruce, rubbing his short gray beard. Maybe he felt uncomfortable with the arrangement of my meeting with the Onyxpaw Pack. Either way, we needed to talk about it. But right now, I wanted to continue shopping for my jewelry and makeup. And at least have fun doing that.

After shopping, we sat in the food court, eating a small breakfast.

I was eating a croissant while the guys had donuts. The croissant was a nice treat after having to walk around all day in the mall. It was a massive mall, with the makeup store being two floor down. We managed to find matching blue jewelry, and I also picked up a few makeup supplies I needed to fully impress the pack that was coming over later.

"Do you need to get anything else?" asked Nick, taking a big bite of his chocolate donut.

"I don't think so," I said. "You guys helped me so much to help make my dreams come true."

"It will happen for you. I can feel it," said Nick. I wasn't sure if he meant it or if he was excited about making money from our match. My heart fluttered again, at the thought of meeting them.

"Not with that pack," interjected Bruce. My heart sank when I realized he wasn't happy about me meeting the Onyxpaw Pack. Then he asked the question I was dreading. "Didn't you feel a connection with me at the Omega Ball? I'm confused, Jade. Is this what you really want?"

Nick's face turned pink as he tried to deflect what Bruce said.

"Don't mind him. He's just a little jealous..." Nick was saying.

"It's okay, Nick," I said, setting down my croissant and turning to Bruce. "I did have a connection with you that night. I'm not going to lie and deny that."

"So what happened then? Why did you sign up for Enchanted Nests?"

There was rising tension in the air. He wasn't happy at all, and I could feel the depth of my rejection of him in this moment.

"I was about to get evicted from my home," I said.

"So this is about money," he replied, disappointed and shaking his head.

"I didn't save much as a nurse because I was using it to pay for my business," I explained. "I quit my job without thinking things through. Actually, I did, but I didn't care because the job was so stressful. Yes, I want a pack who will take care of me and that's my choice."

"Thank you for making that clear," said Bruce, not meeting my eyes.

For some reason, this conversation felt painful to me. My chest hurt as I took a bite of the croissant which felt dry in my throat now. I wanted Bruce to be okay with me. To still talk to me, even though we only met for a few hours. Seeing his good morning text made my heart flutter, and I would never see that again. I would never be able to dance in his arms again.

I wasn't sure if he could be a soulmate of mine. But, if he was, then no power in the universe would separate us. And that's how I saw it.

"Can you imagine being Caleb's mate?" said Nick. I could tell he was trying to lighten the conversation and the heaviness around it.

"Being Caleb's mate would be a disaster," I said, even though inside, I enjoyed being taken care of last night. He took care of every little thing for me. It was for the best, though because I would get ultra-spoiled.

"I grew up in a large family," said Nick. "I wish Caleb could get his act together and finally pick an omega. I crave to have lots of children, just like Bruce here. But, if things don't work out between you and the Onyxpaw Pack, keep us in mind."

When he winked at me, I blushed – unable to believe what he just said.

# Chapter 9

### Jade

"You look amazing," said Caleb upon entering the room I was in. Well, his room, precisely.

When I first came back from the shopping trip, he didn't greet me. Instead, he was holed up in his office all day, a stark contrast from yesterday when he couldn't take his hands off me at bathtime.

"Thanks," I said, putting on the finishing touches of my pink lipstick. I wore my new dress and the jewelry I bought with Nick and Bruce.

"My friend will help tow your car out of the mud tomorrow morning," said Caleb. "It was tough getting ahold of him since he's so busy, but it was the earliest he could do."

"That's okay," I said. "How much is it?"

"I'm not allowing you to pay for it," said Caleb. "I'm touched that you offered. But I am your host, and I'm more than happy to pay for the services."

It felt so weird to have alphas pay for my things and not hesitate.

"I'm grateful for the help," I said. "Really, I am."

It was in the afternoon, and I was getting nervous. The Onyxpaw Pack would be showing up soon. The smell of Dravin's cooking floated upstairs, making my stomach growl, while Nick and Bruce helped him prepare lunch for my big meeting with the alphas.

"Are you nervous? I can sense your fear from here," muttered Caleb, coming up behind me and also gazing at me in the mirror. Caleb was dressed in a professional-looking suit, ready for business. Ready to sell me off to a wealthy alpha pack.

"A little," I said. "How many are there?"

"It's three of them," said Caleb. "A modest pack."

"Okay," I said. So I would need to juggle three males at once. I started envisioning how it would work in the bed and swallowed hard. Then I heard the doorbell ring, and my heart was racing a mile a minute. "Oh my god, they're here."

"I'll greet them. You can come down after a couple of minutes when they settle in, and they can take a good look at your beauty," said Caleb, giving me a once-over. "Everything matters right now. First impressions. Everything."

"Oh hell," I said, holding my stomach.

"Just be yourself," he said. "But not as blunt. Act nice and innocent."

Then Caleb quickly made his way out of the room, his unbuttoned suit swishing behind him. The butterflies in my stomach grew worse the longer I hung out here. I paced around the room, taking long deep breaths trying to calm myself down. The rain was still coming down, but the roads weren't as flooded like yesterday. It was a steady rain with the occasional thunder.

After working up some courage, I left Caleb's room and focused one step at a time down the stairs. I couldn't bring myself to look at the Onyxpaw Pack but I could feel their gazes as I tried to walk down the stairs elegantly. This could be my one and only chance to snag a nice wealthy pack who'd take care of me and love me.

It would be one hell of a dream come true.

When I reached the bottom of the stairs, I saw that they were all sitting on the couch in the living room. All three of them stood up instantaneously to greet me.

"Hello," I said, my voice coming out in a squeak. My hand was shaking as I shook the first one's hand. He was the biggest of the pack, with short brown hair and a mole on his cheek.

"Hello. The beautiful Jade," he said, his voice silky smooth, and my heart beat faster. He had chocolate brown eyes and looked like a businessman with his tailored blue suit and black tie. "I'm Hanibal."

"Nice to meet you," I said.

"I'm Brent," said the second alpha, who had slicked black hair and shiny, gelled eyebrows. I looked at Nick who waggled his own eyebrows. I wanted to laugh but kept a straight face as I shook his hand. I needed to be less picky and more open-minded. He could end up being the love of my life after all. And that thought alone made me burst into a smile.

"Is something funny?" asked Hanibal, also smiling. "I'd like to share in the joke."

"No, it's just..." I said, my voice trailing off as I shook the third alpha's hand, avoiding his question. The third alpha had short hair and a mustache. He looked to be in his forties.

"I'm Nicholas," he said. "Nice to meet you."

"Nice to meet you, too," I said.

"You are very beautiful," said Nicholas, hitching his glasses up and gazing at my hourglass shape created by the dress. I didn't know how to feel about all this. I didn't necessarily feel the instant attraction to this pack like I had with Caleb's pack. But I was still hopeful I'd learn to like them as time passed.

"Let's have some lunch," said Caleb, gesturing towards the large spread on the dining room table fit for sixteen people. We headed to the table, and Hanibal sat to my right while Brent sat to my left.

On the table was chicken, rice, vegetables and salad. Wow, they worked hard cooking for this occasion. I was impressed by the lengths Caleb's pack would take to seal my purchase.

Caleb's pack sat across from me. My hands were shaking as I tried to pour the food onto my plate, and Hanibal, sensing that, took the spoon from me and made my plate with my requests. He seemed attentive like Caleb, and I liked that already about him. Or maybe deep down I was a hopeless romantic.

"Thank you," I said as Hanibal placed the plate of food before me.

"Of course," said Hanibal. "So tell me about yourself, Jade. I've heard plenty, but I'd love to hear from those pretty lips of yours. Tell me about your family."

"I have one brother," I said, almost choking on the rice. It was like I'd forgotten how to speak. I was usually so confident at my workplace around my female friends.

"Do you still live with your family?"

"No, I live alone in an apartment," I said. "I worked as a nurse for years."

"Why did you feel the need to live alone? Wouldn't it corrupt an omega to stay alone?" asked Nicholas, wiping his mustache with a napkin.

*Wow, he was a tool.*

"I needed my independence," I said. "Just like how an alpha leaves his family home and forms his pack. Wouldn't I be afforded the same freedoms in this day and age?"

Caleb's eyes were on his plate, and his jaw was tense.

I didn't care if I embarrassed him. If the Onyxpaw Pack were going to take me, they would have to accept everything about me.

"Of course," said Hanibal in his silky voice, trying to soothe me. "Nicholas didn't mean anything by his question."

I nodded, biting my lip tersely. I took a sip of water to quench my dry throat. It was awkwardly quiet for ten minutes, with only the sounds of chewing and forks clinking on plates.

Nick cleared his throat a couple of times uncomfortably to break the silence.

"How was the rain outside?" I asked, unable to believe I resorted to talking about the weather. "The weather is pretty terrible to travel in."

"We would travel through mountains and ice to meet our intended omega," said Hanibal.

"Oh wow," I said. He was smooth, and I could feel my guard lower around him. Then he asked the next question out of the blue. A question that threw me for a loop.

"Are you a virgin?"

I looked back and forth across the table. Wondering if I had to answer that question, and Caleb gave me a slight nod, signaling that I should answer.

"No," I said, my heart beating fast. Hanibal's eyebrows flew up, and Nicholas made a disapproving noise.

64

"Well, it was nice meeting you," said Hanibal, quickly getting up, not even finishing his food.

*What?!*

The rest of his pack followed suit as they abandoned their full plates of food and walked out of the front door. When the front door flew open, rain rushed inside, wetting the doormat. I sat there in shock. Unable to believe what just happened.

*They had a problem with my virginity?!*

"Damn," said Dravin. "They're fucking idiots."

"We're cutting them from the contract," said Caleb darkly. "I thought we did a thorough background check."

My eyes burned with my impending tears. I couldn't cry over a pack I just met. For the next few minutes, I tried to eat with Caleb's pack pretending nothing had happened. But I couldn't take it anymore.

"Um, excuse me for a second," I whispered, getting up from my chair.

"Jade, please eat your food," said Bruce softly, his eyes on me.

"I'll be back," I said, turning and heading up the stairs. I hoped they didn't see the hint of my tears as I rushed up the last steps. Then, heading into Caleb's room, I sat on the bed and finally let the tears flow.

Rejection hurt like a bitch. Especially to an omega.

We would preen ourselves and look pretty for alphas. But when they reject us, even if I just met them, it cut a hole through my heart. Looking around the room, I needed a more enclosed space. A space that felt like a hug.

I went into the closet and leaned against Caleb's many suits and his stack of watches.

Every time I wiped my tears away, more flowed down like a river. I couldn't help it. I just wanted a pack that adored every inch of me. I was a little crazy in my past, but that shouldn't deter them from wanting me.

I sniffled, trying to catch my breath.

My chest felt tight like I wouldn't be able to breathe normally again. The way they looked at me in disgust and left was the most embarrassing thing to ever happen to me. In front of everyone too. It was way worse than standing naked in front of a pack of alphas.

"Are you okay in there?" asked Caleb from outside the door.

# Chapter 10

### Caleb

I felt bad for this innocent omega.

She didn't do anything to the Onxypaw Pack, and yet they treated her like garbage. It bothered me to no end, and I vowed to fucking take revenge. They would not hear the end of it, and I would make sure they didn't try to join another dating agency ever again.

"Please give me a moment," she said in a shaky voice.

She was in the closet. Omegas craved small enclosed spaces when they were emotional, nesting, or in heat. I respected that, but I had to go in there. This disaster was completely my fault.

"We should have done better," said Bruce, shaking his head.

"Don't blame yourself," said Dravin, clapping me on the shoulder.

I opened the closet door, seeing her small form curled up under my suits hanging above her. I was going in there, whether she liked it or not.

"Please go away," she whimpered, covering her face with her hands, and turning towards the wall. Her wavy black hair came out of its bun, tumbling down her back and down the blue dress she was so excited to wear today. I gently placed my hand on her shoulder, trying not to startle her.

She didn't move or flinch when I touched her.

"Jade," I said. She slowly turned around and uncovered her face. It was obvious that she was crying. This meeting had broken her heart.

"You said my name," she whispered, looking confused.

"You're not just any random omega," I said. "Today wasn't your fault at all, Jade. I will find a pack worthy of your attention."

Jade looked down, her face falling.

"What is it?" asked Bruce, crowding in next to us.

"I don't want to go through this process again," she said. "To get my hopes up and then crushed because I'm not a virgin."

I was curious about her past and who in the hell she slept with. And who she deemed worthy. But it didn't matter to me at all.

"If it had worked out, you would have been stuck with the gelled eyebrows guy, Brent," said Nick.

His comment made her smile, and I was glad it did. She would get over this.

Eventually.

After lots of comforting and hugging her, we managed to pull her away from the closet and onto the bed. Nick and Dravin sat on either side of her. Nick dabbed at her tears with a tissue, and Dravin purred into her ear. *Damn, my pack is ready to take care of an omega*. But I couldn't take on a new omega. I wasn't ready.

"I'll be back," I told them. They were too entranced with Jade, and that wasn't good at all. We would lose potential business.

When I left the room and went downstairs, I noticed Bruce had followed me. Bruce's whole demeanor changed. He looked anxious and upset for some reason.

"I think we should keep her," he said.

"Are you talking about Jade?"

"Of course. Who the fuck else would I be talking about? Stop dodging the question, Caleb."

I rubbed my eyes. It had been a tiresome failure of a day, and I lost a cool million-dollar deal already.

"I'm not ready to take on a new omega," I explained for the hundredth time.

"But we are. It's been five years since Glenda was murdered," said Bruce, with no mercy in his eyes. "We need to move on and take a new wife."

My heart ached at the sound of her name, but it wasn't as bad as it had been when it was fresh. I found her in our backyard, completely mutilated by something wild. Found with wolf claw marks all over her. Her body was nearly unrecognizable. I failed at my job of protecting her.

And I wasn't going to let that happen again.

"We cannot," I said, shaking my head.

Bruce let out an audible sigh. "If you're not taking on an omega anytime soon- I'm not sure I want to stay in this pack any longer."

*What the fuck was he thinking?* Leaving a pack was unheard of in Howl's Edge.

"A pack stays together and loyal to whatever the pack leader decides," I said, hackles rising. "I don't need to tell you that, Bruce."

"I need time to think," said Bruce, leaving out the front door without another word. "You're being unreasonable."

He was the most emotional alpha I ever met, but his heart was in the right place. He was frustrated with me, but I would give him time to cool off. He would be back.

And if not...I would be furious if he left over an omega.

"Hey Ma," I said, walking in through the front door of the guesthouse when she didn't answer the door.

I had a plate of food from Dravin's feast, and I wanted her to have some even though she isolated herself from people living in this tiny house. It was a two-room building with a modest pink couch in the living room with a fireplace. She had hung curtains everywhere to block all sunlight. I couldn't find her in the living room or her bedroom.

Looking in the second room, I saw her sitting cross-legged on the ground in her patterned dress, surrounded by candles and a marking of a circle around her. Her dreadlocks were covered in multi-colored beads, and her face was shiny with sweat.

She was mumbling something under her breath.

I never believed in her witchery magic shenanigans, but the people of Howl's Edge seemed to trust my mother, Zaneesha.

"Hello, son," she said in a scratchy voice, resting her hands on her knees. She turned to me slowly, as if it took all her energy.

"Mom, what's wrong?" I asked, kneeling outside of her circle of candles in the dark room. The shadows from the flames danced around the room. "I've brought you food. It's on the kitchen counter."

"I'm being weakened by the Shadow Wolf," she said quietly. "Ever since it left the sigma that I entrapped him with. He's not contained anymore."

The Shadow Wolf was her imagination of a demon. Something I never understood. But from the stories she told me, she had summoned him to help save Howl's Edge Island years ago. My dad had passed away on my tenth birthday. Even though my mother was an omega, she only had one mate, which was unheard of. Nobody questioned her because of how much she helped everyone on the island. She did her own thing as an omega.

"Are you saying the Shadow Wolf's here?"

"Yes," she shuddered. "This circle of protection can only last so long. I fear he may take over me."

"You need to leave this house, Ma," I said. "Maybe some fresh air will help. Nothing is going to take over you."

"I know you never believed in this stuff," she said, looking off to the corner as if she could actually see the Shadow Wolf. She wiped her forehead with a rag. "I cannot leave this circle until I can find a way."

"This is ridiculous. You're getting weaker every day. Please live in the house with me at least," I said. "You can have my room until we can move into the mansion I purchased last week for us."

"I don't want to put you in danger," she said. Her excuse for years was that she needed to be alone to do her business and didn't want to be around anyone else's toxic energy. "I saw your omega the other day. She's very pretty."

"Yeah, she's not ours, though," I said, giving up on trying to convince her to live a normal life with me. My mother was the only blood relative I had left in this world, and I didn't want to see her expire this way.

"Why not?"

"I'm matching her up with a pack. She's been looking for a long time for the right pack."

"What if *you* are the pack for her?"

"I'll think about it," I said to stop her from prying. I had enough discussing Jade for one day.

"Can you please bring the food in here?"

"Yes, of course," I said, leaving the room. I needed her to eat something. She looked ill and didn't look like her usual self at all. Her skin had a yellow tinge to it, and her eyes were baggy from lack of sleep.

It was only a matter of time before I would have to drag her to the hospital. Her mental health was slowly declining, despite what the people thought. I believed she could concoct herbal remedies for people but not magical powers. It was too far-fetched for me to believe. I wasn't around when she conjured up this mythical Shadow Wolf, and I wasn't there when she helped various people with their problems.

I needed to get her the help she needed before I lost her too.

# Chapter 11

## Jade

"How many males do you prefer for your future pack?" asked Caleb.

Later that night, we were all sitting in the living room while Caleb drilled me with questions of what I would be looking for in my perfect match. He seemed remorseful about the Onyxpaw Pack, but I didn't blame him.

None of us could have foreseen what would have happened. But this time he was determined to match me with the pack of my dreams, and I was hopeful he would find one. Bruce wasn't around either for some reason, and Caleb wasn't answering any questions regarding him.

"Four, but the max I'd take is eight," I said bluntly. Dravin sitting next to me on the couch smirked at my answer. "What's so funny? An omega has needs."

"Nothing's funny," he said hastily when I glared at him.

"All alphas?"

"A mix is fine," I said. "It would be nice to have a sensitive beta in the pack and maybe a hot delta or two."

"What's wrong with all alphas?" asked Nick.

*God, these alphas.* It was the precise reason why I couldn't have all alphas.

"Guys, these are her choices. No need to take any of this personally," said Caleb. Then he placed his clipboard on the coffee table and tapped his pen to his lips. "I'm curious too, though. Would an entire pack of only alphas be enough?"

"Yes," I said. "Nothing wrong with an entire pack of all alphas. It's just nice to have a variety mix."

Dravin guffawed at my answer, and Caleb's lips quirked into a smile.

"Let's have some fun now," said Nick. "Our guest is probably tired of all the questions."

"I don't mind," I said. "Whatever helps me get matched."

It wasn't that late at night, so it was too early for bed. Tomorrow, Caleb would take me to my car, and I would finally be in my home. So this would be my last night here.

"Let's play a game or something," said Dravin.

"How about a board game?" I suggested. I was bored out of my mind sitting on this couch getting interviewed all day. This pack was mostly business-minded and needed to let loose sometimes.

"What?" said Caleb.

"I love the idea," said Nick. "Tapping into my inner child."

"Uhhh," said Dravin. "How about truth or dare?"

"Okay," I said, tucking my feet under me, on the couch. I was still wearing my blue dress since I only had Caleb's shirt to wear to sleep. There was no way I was going to run around this house in just the shirt and underwear.

"I'll go first," said Nick, his eyes gleaming with excitement.

"Truth or dare?" asked Dravin.

"Truth."

"How many omegas have you slept with?"

"Two," answered Nick. "Our pack wife, Glenda, and another during my teens."

My mouth fell open.

"You have a pack wife?" I asked. In my head, I entertained the idea of them possibly being my pack. I thought about it late last night and would get horny as hell before I slept. Unfortunately, I was growing a little too attached and needed to pull away immediately.

"Not anymore," said Caleb in a hoarse voice. His face looked pained. "She passed away."

"I'm sorry," I said, meaning it. I could feel the pain and the emotion ricocheting off the alphas. This was clearly a topic they didn't delve into often, and I didn't want to stir up old pains.

"Well, let's continue," said Dravin, clearing his throat. "Your turn Jade. Truth or dare?"

"Dare," I said, my heart pounding.

"Hmm...," said Dravin, suddenly getting a wild look in his eyes. His breathing turned harsher, and his short red hair looked electric. "I dare you to hide, and we will all look for you. If we find you in one minute, you will sit here naked with your legs spread for pictures. Don't worry, we'll delete it afterward."

"Are you fucking serious?!"

I could feel my slick coating my pussy at his wild idea.

"We'll give you a twenty-second head start," said Dravin.

"One, two," said Caleb, licking his lips.

Nick grinned with excitement.

I immediately stood up and started running across the house as the alphas laughed in the living room. My heart was pounding hard as I searched for the perfect hiding spot. I needed to be in a good spot for just one minute. I ran to every room, trying to find any nook or cranny. I ran into the bathroom, than ran back out.

I went to Dravin's room, and it was messy as hell. Blankets were thrown on the ground, and his clothes were scattered all over the place.

I dived into his closet, scurrying all the way to the back.

Pulling his large black jacket in front of me, I felt like I was covered enough. I didn't have time to pull the closet door shut when I heard their heavy footsteps pounding up the stairs.

*Fuck*. I tried to breathe as slowly as possible.

Dravin's strong alpha scent surrounded me, disguising my natural scent.

"Where are you, little omega?" called Caleb down the hall, intensifying my panic. "Scared to get naked in front of us again?"

"I can't wait to see her little pussy spread," cackled Dravin.

"That would be hot," said Nick. "I'm already hard, man."

My pussy twitched, and my breathing grew more erratic. This is what happened if an omega was in a house trapped for too long with a bunch of alphas. I pressed my hand between my legs to suppress any scent from my vagina. Footsteps came into the room, and I held my breath. I counted to twenty seconds in my head. I just had to stay hidden for a little longer. I didn't dare make a move.

Suddenly I heard his voice in my right ear.

"I know when the scent of my room changes," whispered Dravin, standing behind me in the closet. I couldn't believe he snuck in so fast. I didn't hear him or sense him. My back was pressed against his chest, and he wrapped his arm around me, pressing his hand to my belly.

Caleb and Nick were still looking for me in the other rooms, calling my name and teasing me.

My body was growing hot at the contact with Dravin's body, and my pulse had skyrocketed.

"Please let me win," I whispered.

"Hmm," he said, his fingers pulling my dress up. I swallowed nervously as his hand trailed up my bare leg underneath my dress. His fingers stopped just at my pussy. I was getting wetter and more excited with every second that his fingers were there. "Your panties are drenched. Why is that?"

His fingers slid underneath the fabric against my naked pussy.

"I don't know," I whispered, trying to keep him there for another minute so I could win the game. But I also enjoyed his fingers.

I heard footsteps entering the room, and I held my breath as Dravin's finger pressed against my clitoris, teasing it. Pressing and releasing like he was playing with a button on a remote.

"Come out, little omega," said Caleb. "We want to see your shaved pussy. If it's hairy again, I'll take care of it for you tonight."

More slick dripped from me as my pussy clenched. Then I heard his footsteps leaving the room.

Dravin pressed a finger inside my pussy and whispered in my ear as I bucked in his hand. His thick finger spread me wide.

"*Shh*, or else he'll find you."

His finger pressed deeper into my pussy, and I clamped a hand to my mouth. It felt so good and so right. His middle finger sunk in deeper inside me, sending my body into a craze. I wanted something way bigger. His alpha knot deep inside me. His finger stilled inside me, not moving, as he chuckled softly behind me.

But he wasn't my alpha.

"Please," I begged, not caring if Caleb or Nick caught me.

"Do you want my finger to fuck you hard?" he asked, still not moving his finger. My pussy clenched tight around his finger, begging him. "You're slick is all over my finger. You're not allowed to come until I say so, baby."

I grasped his arm in desperation, willing his finger to move.

Until he did.

He fingered me like it was no one's business, pumping in and out of me. Two fingers were inside me now, stretching me, thrusting wildly. He reached around with his other hand and rubbed my clit. It felt amazing having his two sausage fingers pumping deep inside me while he strummed my clit. My breathing grew labored as I waited for the incoming orgasm. My eyes rolled back as I took it all in. Dravin's rough breathing and his hard cock pressing against my butt.

Then I shattered, coming hard all over his fingers. My body quaked, and my legs shook as I tried to stand. He pulled me against his body so I didn't fall as I tried to catch my breath.

"I found her!" shouted Dravin, shocking me.

Footsteps pounded into the room, and Caleb ripped the coat away, revealing my red face. I tried to slow down my breathing, but the smirk on his face showed that he knew exactly what happened.

"How long ago did you find the little omega?"

"Thirty seconds in the game. Don't act like you didn't know we were in here."

"So you lost, dear Jade," said Caleb with a smile.

"No, he tricked me," I protested, covering myself.

"It's time for you to strip then," Caleb ordered me. "We would all like to look at your dripping pussy that I allowed Dravin to cause."

"What?!" I said.

"It's much better for photos," said Dravin. "You chose the dare."

Realizing I'd been tricked, I stepped out of the closet and slowly removed my dress.

"Panties and bra off too," said Nick, his eyes wide.

"You guys have already seen me before," I said as I stood there. My panties were drenched, and I was ashamed for them to see my pussy after it had been ravaged by Dravin's fingers. Instead, they stood there expectantly, arms crossed and watching me closely.

I rolled off my underwear and unsnapped my bra.

"Go to the living room," said Dravin. "Remember the dare? You need to sit on the couch naked."

All this was turning me on all over again. The leakage from my pussy dripped down my thighs as I walked down the stairs, with them following close behind as I clutched my clothes in one hand. I could feel their gazes on my ass as I walked.

"She has such a beautiful bouncy ass," said Dravin.

"She does," said Nick, and I felt warmth flow through my entire body.

When we got to the living room, I sat on the edge of the couch, covering my privates with my hand.

"Not what we agreed at all," said Dravin. Then he placed his hands on my hips and positioned me comfortably against the couch. "Are you chickening out now? Or will you spread your legs so we can all take a look? Do you concede defeat?"

Annoyed now, I angrily spread my legs so he didn't think he had won.

"I don't mind at all," I said, spreading my legs wide so they could take a look.

"Damn," said Nick, pulling his cell phone out for a picture. They were standing around me. Their hulking alpha forms towered above me as they gazed at my pussy. My scent filled the room, and I was embarrassed I was perfuming so much.

"Look how her pussy is dripping," said Dravin. "Are you guys jealous I was able to stick my fingers in there?"

"Yes," said Nick, leaning closer for another picture.

"How long am I supposed to stay like this?" I asked, turned on and self-conscious. Dravin gripped his dick through his pants.

"Until we tell you," said Dravin.

I heard the front door open, and before I could close my legs, Bruce barged in.

"What the fuck?" said Bruce, seeing me spread wide and open for the alphas.

# Chapter 12

### Jade

Scrambling up, I closed my legs and pulled my dress over my exposed breasts.

"Dude, we're playing truth or dare," growled Dravin.

"You ruined the fun," sighed Nick, a visible erection in his pants.

They all sat around the couch like we had before we started playing the game. My heart was still beating fast, and I was still aroused.

"Looks like someone's back," muttered Caleb, looking at Bruce as he plopped onto the big chair.

Bruce walked over to me and stood next to me protectively. His shirt and pants were wet from the rain outside. His face looked livid.

"Are you alphas toying with her?" he asked darkly. Then he turned to me. "Did you want to be part of our pack?"

"I mean," I stuttered. "I...I wouldn't mind."

"Do you, Caleb, want Jade to join our pack? She's not some common omega to play with," said Bruce, turning on his heel to face Caleb.

I also looked at Caleb to see what he would say. Butterflies swirled around my belly, and I wanted to throw up. I wasn't sure what I wanted him to say.

Caleb didn't say anything as he stared down at Bruce. His jaw was tensing, and I knew that was a no.

Biting my lip, I slowly got up and calmly pulled my dress over my head. I felt like a fool getting naked so many times with them. They weren't remotely attracted to a chubby omega like myself. They were probably looking for a supermodel omega, considering how good-looking these alphas are.

*When was I ever going to learn?*

"I just wanted to thank you guys for letting me stay," I said after I had the dress on messily.

I had to say something to break the awkward silence.

They were all looking at me with pity in their eyes, and I just wanted to run. I wanted to fucking run out of here and never come back. My throat was tight, and I willed myself to hold back the tears. I couldn't cry a second time today over rejection. For some reason, this one hurt more. I spent time with these alphas, and it was near impossible not to get attached.

Before I could take a step, Caleb stalked over to me and pulled me onto his lap on the couch. His heavy breathing in my ear made me stay still. His feral side was coming out, and I had no idea why it was provoked.

He was the one rejecting *me*.

"The reason why I can't have you," he said as he cupped my pussy over my dress. "I would protect every inch of you. You would be completely mine. I messed up before not protecting my past wife, and I won't make that mistake again."

"What are you talking about?" I asked, squirming on his lap. His body felt warm and hard underneath me, taunting me with what was near but so far.

"If you were my omega," he said, grasping my breasts. "I would bathe you, feed you, carry you everywhere. And no omega wants that."

I gulped. This was a lot.

Something was clearly wrong with him to feel that overprotective.

"Maybe you're right," I said, pulling away from him, and he released me. "I like my freedom, and I think I'll keep it that way."

His eyes darkened.

"Just like I thought. You're not my type Jade."

"That's fine. I'll take a taxi," I said. "Thank you all again. Bye Nick, Bruce, and Dravin."

I didn't even wait for their reply before I rushed out the door with my phone in my hand. I needed out of there. It was still raining, and my ankles instantly got wet. I didn't care right now. I had to get to my cozy apartment and away from these fucking alphas.

It was pitch dark outside.

I was walking fast in the general direction of the road. I needed to use the flashlight from my phone. As I fumbled with my phone, I suddenly dropped my phone into the water.

"Damn it," I muttered, bending down to feel for it on the ground. I couldn't see a damn thing in the night. Then, suddenly, I heard a harsh whisper in my ear.

*"You're mine, bitch."*

My heart jumped in my throat. Freezing midway, I heard the voice veer off into a loud cackle.

"Who's that? Is that you Caleb?" I said loudly, my heart racing.

Chills went down my spine. There had to be someone out here. The top of my right arm felt like it was burning, and I screamed.

There was something out here attacking me. Ditching my phone, I started running back toward the house but crashed into someone.

"Jade! Are you okay?" asked Caleb, shining a bright flashlight into my face. His face was twisted in concern, wondering why I was screaming like a mad woman.

"Something just attacked me," I shouted, breathless and grabbing my arm. The burning was still there, but it had died down a little bit. "My arm."

He shined the flashlight onto my shaky arm, and I was horrified to see four long scratches on it. Like wolf claw marks.

His face suddenly turned white as he shined the flashlight everywhere. To my shock, nothing was there.

"I need to get you out of here," he rasped. *He knew what it was.*

"Wait, my phone fell in the water," I said.

He helped me locate my phone with his flashlight, and then he grabbed my hand - quickly leading me toward his truck. There was something out here that he wasn't telling me about.

"Get in," he said, opening the passenger door for me, and I quickly hopped inside. I couldn't stop staring at my arm. It was unbelievable. Could it have been an alpha in his shifted state? But it didn't explain the creepy voice. It couldn't have been an alpha whispering and then shifting in a matter of seconds. That was impossible. At least from what I knew.

Caleb climbed into the truck, revving the engine the minute he shut the door.

"Where do you live?" he asked.

"Down King's Aisle Street. Maybridge Apartments," I said.

"Got it," he said. The island wasn't that big, and he would know the general area at least.

"Do you know what attacked me?" I asked. He silently zoomed down the road, intent on getting the hell out of there. "Caleb? You clearly know what it is, but you're not telling me. Do you have a pet wolf or something? Tell me!"

"I didn't tell you how our wife died," he said. "She was found with claw marks and mutilated beyond recognition."

My hand flew to my mouth.

"Oh my god," I said. "That's so horrible. I'm sorry."

"It was five years ago," Caleb continued. "We had only been married for six months. We left her just one night to have a alphas' night out so she could relax at home and...well, I paid for it dearly. I made a vow to never, ever do that again. I abandoned our omega at the time that she was the most scared. The time she needed her alphas the most. I will never forgive myself."

No wonder he was overprotective and overbearing. His past had left a scar on him. I was starting to understand his fear now of taking on a new omega. The huge responsibility on his shoulders for his new mate.

I didn't know what to say. I've never had to deal with the death of anyone close to me. But simply imagining his pain made me want to bawl. I looked at the scratches on my arm, bleeding down my dress. He handed me a tissue, and I held it to my wound.

"Mistakes happen in life," I said. "Who or what do you think could have attacked her?"

"I have no idea," he said. "Glenda was such an introvert. She didn't have any friends, really, just family. I can't think of anyone who would want to attack her so violently."

"I can't even imagine," I said, cradling my arm and pressing the tissue against it. This wasn't my imagination. The scratch was clearly there, and there was a voice before it attacked me. I didn't want to tell him about the voice and what it said. It was too bizarre and I would sound insane.

I turned my phone on, hoping it would still work after being submerged in water for so long. After a couple of minutes, it finally lit up, and I was relieved. Pulling up my text messages, I realized I hadn't texted any of my friends back for several hours and had missed calls from Keera. When I got home, I was prepared to tell the girls my sob story and what happened. They were so excited that I was finally going to get matched to a pack, and it still hadn't happened.

I felt like such a failure.

"Now that I've disclosed nearly all my secrets," said Caleb, glancing over at me while driving. "Tell me about your past dating life. It's not often that an omega isn't a virgin."

It was true. Omegas were supposed to save themselves for an alpha pack. We were the only ones capable of producing alpha babies on Howl's Edge. I lost my virginity out of the spur of the moment and because I couldn't resist a particular alpha.

"I didn't date often," I said. "I lost my virginity during a masked party seven years ago when I was twenty-one- masquerading as a beta girl."

"Hmm, a masked party?" he asked inquisitively, looking at me- his eyebrows rising as he looked back at the road.

"Yeah, it was a random Halloween party for crazy college kids," I said. "I don't even remember the guy. But I remember the tattoo of a leaf between his shoulders on his back. We were so drunk, I could barely remember it. It's whatever. I was gone by the time he woke up, but it was one hell of a good knotting."

Caleb's arms suddenly tensed on the steering wheel.

"Are you sure?" he asked, turning to me.

"Sure, what?"

"That the tattoo was a leaf?"

All of a sudden, my hands turned clammy, and my face became hot.

"Yes," I whispered.

"That's me. It was me who you slept with that night."

# Chapter 13

### Caleb

"What the hell," groaned Jade, holding her face between her hands as she leaned forward on her lap.

I couldn't believe it.

I was looking for this omega for a full two years before I met Glenda, who was the next best thing at the time. I settled, but we had gradually grown into an understanding. My heart raced as I tried not to stare at Jade and crash the truck. I wanted to look at her again.

I remembered how magnetic her pull was at the party. Her sleek red mask and red dress. Her subtle sexuality pulled me in even deeper. It was a like a gut punch when I found her gone a couple of hours after we made love on the roof. Her being still pulled my heart to this day.

And even now. No matter how hard I tried to fight it.

Jade had lingered on my mind, and it was but a distant memory now. My heart beat hard in my chest, remembering her beautiful thick thighs and soft belly as I kissed her body that night. I couldn't believe I didn't recognize those thighs of hers. I literally masturbated the other night, staring at her legs and her pussy.

"I won't talk about it if you don't want to," I said, placing my hand on her thigh. She tensed, and I pulled my hand back. I didn't want to make her uncomfortable.

"It's crazy that we met before," she said softly, slowly lifting her face and looking at me. "No wonder your scent was familiar to me."

I kept my eyes on the road to avoid making her feel more self-conscious than she already was. I could smell her scent rising, turning into the scent of sour green apple from her nervousness. I tried to avoid inhaling her scent, but it was impossible in the truck. She hadn't worn scent blockers in a while, so her perfume intoxicated me. I wanted to pull the truck to the side of the road and fuck her until the morning. Ram my dick into her until she screamed my name.

But I couldn't do that. Bruce was right.

We shouldn't string this omega along if we weren't going to be serious.

"I looked for you that night," I said. "I searched for the girl in the red mask and heels for a long time."

"You're lying," she whispered, staring out the window.

"Why would I lie to you? That night was special to me," I said. "We had a connection that I can remember even today. Before we fucked, we talked and laughed for hours. Don't you remember?"

"I remember," she whispered, pressing the tissue against her wound. It hurt me that she was hurt. "Because you thought I was a beta, and we both wanted a one-night stand sort of thing."

"It was more than that," I said, parking the car at her residence. "No wonder you caught my eye at the Omega Ball."

She laughed.

"Well, it was a long time ago," she said. "Things happen over the

89

years, and people change."

## Jade

"Here we are," said Caleb, turning off the engine.

"It's okay. I can walk myself to the door," I protested. It was awkward enough being in the truck with him after his admission. His presence was too much for me, and I was overwhelmed. I didn't know what to think.

"I'll walk you to the door," said Caleb without hesitation as he hopped out of the truck.

We walked to the apartment, and I was sort of glad I was getting back to my normal life. I missed my room, art, and routine. I spent more than enough time vacationing with a bunch of alphas in their home. Things had gotten too sexual and out of control over there. It was for the best.

"Whoa, what are those boxes?" asked Caleb as we made our way to my door.

"No idea," I said, walking past the six boxes piled high on top of each other. I took my keys out and inserted it into the lock on my door. The lock wouldn't twist open. *What the heck?* "I can't open the damn door."

"Is this yours?" asked Caleb, and I turned to see him holding my pink vibrator by the rubber handle in his hands with a smirk on his face. My face heated instantly, and I snatched it from him. In a panic, I quickly rummaged through the box in the hallway, and sure enough, they were my things. My underwear, lingerie, and accessories were in this box. My paintings were leaning against the wall, put carelessly there. They were each worth a few hundred dollars.

*Yep.* I was officially evicted.

I opened another box containing all my clothes from my closet. The next box had all my kitchen stuff.

"I had two days left to pay the rent," I said, staring at the boxes and feeling like my world was collapsing under me. "I completely forgot while I was staying with you guys."

I quit my job and now this. I could beg the landlady to give me a few more days, but I highly doubted she would care.

"Do you have family to stay with? I'll help you take the boxes, and I can give you a ride there," offered Caleb. He didn't sound judgmental that I was homeless now and he genuinely wanted to help.

I didn't want to go back to live with my parents. They would dictate my life again, even though they thought they were giving me all the freedom for an omega. I started hyperventilating, my breaths coming in short gasps.

"I'm so fucking stupid," I said, collapsing against the wall and sliding down.

"Why?" said Caleb, sitting next to me cross-legged. I could feel the heat from his body as his knees were very close to my thighs.

"I should never have quit my job," I groaned. "Now I have to go back to my parents. I have an older brother, but he's mated now with two kids. I can't go there."

"How about any friends?"

"All my friends are mated with kids," I said. "I have no choice but to go back to my mom's house."

"May I ask why you quit your job?"

91

"I had a big gig to help my cousin with her wedding planning which she canceled," I explained. "I have a small business designing rooms, party planning, or selling paintings. I'm pretty much all over the place. Fuck my life."

"Is it that bad?"

I gave him a dead stare, and he chuckled.

"It *is* that bad," I answered. It was humiliating for him to see me like this. I'd rather live on the streets than go back to live with my parents. I loved them but not enough to move back in with them.

"I have an idea that might help," he said.

"Yeah?"

There was nothing that could help me now. I made all my life choices which led to a dead end. And there was no way I could stay at his place.

"I just recently purchased a home and need an interior designer," he started. "Do you think you can help with that?"

"Yes, I definitely can," I breathed, hope lifting inside me. "Believe it or not, I have an eye for interior design."

"Excellent," said Caleb. "For payment, you can stay at the new house until you can secure something for yourself. It'll buy you some time to figure everything out."

"Are you fucking serious?!" I said.

I couldn't believe it. This was the answer to my problems.

"Dead serious," he said. "Let's get your boxes into the truck and head over there."

"Thank you so much, Caleb," I said as I threw myself to him in a hug. He was startled initially but pulled me in for a hug. As if he was apologizing for something. When he released me, I was breathless but happy.

I was given a second chance, and this time I wasn't going to screw it up.

# Chapter 14

## Jade

"This is it," said Caleb as we walked to his new house. It was already nightfall as I carried two smaller boxes while he carried three big boxes between his muscular arms. The new house looked like a mansion, and I couldn't believe my eyes. Even in the dark, I could see how huge the house was. Lights dotted the inside of the mansion.

"Is there someone in there?" I asked.

"Nope, the lights are there to deter anyone looking to crash into my two-million-dollar home," said Caleb, opening the front door.

"The house is beautiful," I said, looking at the ornate statues on the front of the building. There were such weird designs I'd never seen. A large white cube that floated in midair caught my eye. It glowed with a soft light in the dark. The play on lights made it look like it was floating.

The house was huge but empty. Not a speck of furniture or décor in sight, except that the oval-shaped windows framed in crystal.

I followed Caleb across the large living room area and past the two kitchens. We entered a room at the end of the hallway on the first floor. It had a single bed in the middle and a bathroom with a shower. The bathroom door was open with the light switched on. Caleb switched on the light in the room after setting down the boxes in the corner. I dropped the boxes breathlessly onto the messy mattress.

"This will be your room while you're helping us out," he said, straightening back up. "Sorry, the bed is messy. I slept there while renovating the place."

*I somehow always ended up in Caleb's bed.* Maybe it was fate talking, but it was frustrating breathing in his scent and not being able to have him.

"It's okay," I said. "Better than me living in the streets, trust me."

He smiled, his gaze thoughtful as he looked at me.

"Here's the key to the house," he said, setting down a single key on the nightstand. "We all have a copy of the key, so this should work. Also, here is my credit card to go shopping and buy whatever you need for the house."

"Is there a specific style you'd like? A type of sofa or design?"

"I'm not a picky alpha," he said, winking.

"You're only picky with omegas," I said and he chuckled.

"The house can be any design you like," said Caleb. "Anything that makes it a home. Go crazy."

"How much should I spend on your card?"

I wanted to be extra careful and ensure I had all the bases covered. If he fired me for something stupid I did, I couldn't take any chances. I wanted to succeed and showcase my talent to him. He was my biggest client so far.

"There's no limit," he said. The shadow of his sideburns did something to my lady parts. His shoulder-length black hair covered one eye as he gazed at me. The large watch on his wrist glinted off the moonlight. My stomach tensed as I remembered his confession. He was the first and only alpha I've ever slept with.

"Oh wow, okay," I said, carefully placing the card on the house key.

"Buy whatever you need for yourself. Clothes, makeup...whatever an omega needs," he said. "Even though you get to live here as payment- I'll also pay you a small salary every week."

"It's not necessary," I protested.

"You need to be able to afford your own place," he said. "Don't worry. I *want* to help you. It's the least I could do for how we behaved with the game tonight. I'm sorry about that."

"It's okay," I said, looking down.

"It's *not* okay," he said. "We behaved badly tonight with no intention of keeping you. I let my alpha rut hormones control me. We shouldn't have teased you tonight. I had no idea you wanted to be our omega until Bruce asked you that question."

"No, not anymore," I said quickly. "I understand now fully. Don't worry." I actually appreciated him apologizing to me. He wasn't *that* much of a monster.

"That's all for now, it's pretty late," said Caleb. "Call me if you need anything, okay? I'll check on you tomorrow in the afternoon or after I'm done with work."

"Sounds good."

"Alright, see you tomorrow," said Caleb, lingering at the doorway, his eyes on my lips.

"See you," I said softly. When he left the room, I bit my lower lip. My omega self wanted to wrap myself around him. To smell him again.

Hug him tight and let him dominate every inch of me. I couldn't let my mind go there. The darkest parts of me wanted that, but my rational brain wanted me to be successful and take advantage of the opportunity he gave me.

After I heard the front door closing, I sighed and looked at all my boxes.

I began pulling the stacked boxes down and organizing them against the wall, so I could access my things easier. Opening each of them, I dug through them until I could find a clean pair of pajamas and a towel. I wanted to shower and sleep so badly. Then I could daydream about my new job in bed.

The bathroom only had a bar soap in the shower and nothing else. I placed my toothbrush and accessories on the counter. Stripping off my dress and underwear, I hopped into the shower. The water ran cold for a while, which worried me, but eventually warmed up. I needed to buy shower supplies first thing as I used the bar soap. It was so warm and cozy in the shower that I took my sweet time in there, making sure I lathered every inch of my skin.

Wrapping the towel around my chest, I stared into the bathroom mirror as I combed out my long wet hair which was plastered down my face. Blow-drying my hair took forever, as I did that while thinking about my deal with Caleb. I was nervous but also confident that I could do it. I had to assess the living room first thing tomorrow morning to figure out the best style for it.

When I turned off the blow dryer, I heard a loud thud in the living room.

I froze, my heart pounding as I held the blow dryer out like a weapon.

"Who's there?!" I shouted, my voice screechy with fear. No one should be here. It was late at night too. I walked out of the bathroom and into my bedroom. The footsteps came directly down the hall and to my room. It was too late to shut the door as I stared daggers at the doorway, holding my towel tight around me.

Then I saw Bruce standing at the doorway, his gaze on me- slowly looking me up and down. He was wearing a white shirt with grey sweatpants.

"It's just me, don't freak out," he said, smirking when he saw the blow dryer in my hands, which I carefully put down.

Letting out a long breath, I collapsed on the edge of the bed.

"You scared the shit out of me," I said. "What are you doing here?"

"We all have keys to the house, but I'm sorry for coming without warning," he said, walking into the room. "You weren't answering your phone. Caleb told us the big news that you will be our designer."

"Yeah, I was in the shower, and also it's kind of late," I said pointedly, staring at the clock on the nightstand. He could clearly see it was midnight and not a normal time for a social visit.

"I wanted to make sure you were okay," he said, walking towards the boxes and glancing around my room. "Needed to make sure Caleb was treating you right."

"It's not too bad in here," I said, suddenly conscious that I was completely naked under the towel. I kept my thighs together, so I didn't tempt him with my scent. We had to keep things professional now.

I was their hired worker and nothing else.

But I knew he wasn't over it when he looked at me. He wasn't over the connection we had.

His eyes roamed over to the little box that had my vibrator, and I quickly shot up, running over to the box. As I ran, the towel dropped around my ankles, and I gasped, already five feet away from my towel.

Before I could run back for the towel on the ground, Bruce grasped my wrist.

"Hold on," he said slowly, his eyes raking over my naked body. I quickly covered my pussy with my other hand, but he grabbed my other wrist, pulling it away.

"Bruce, no," I said breathlessly, my heart pounding hard with desire. God knows how much this pack sexually teased me, and my pent-up horniness was going to be the cause of my demise. "We can't."

"Why not?" he asked, his eyes darkening. "Caleb may not agree, but I don't give a fuck anymore. I want you as my omega."

Before I could say another word, he smashed his lips over mine, effectively silencing me. My mind was screaming at me, but my body enjoyed his sandalwood scent. His gray beard brushed against me as his lips played over mine. I closed my eyes as I leaned into his body, his strong arms around me. Fires of passion overwhelmed my body and my soul. I wanted this alpha. Ever since day one, he caught my eye. My pussy trembled and clenched, releasing more of my scent into the room.

He pushed me down on the bed on my back, his hands still grasping my wrists. Trapping my hands over my head. He broke the kiss and smiled devilishly at me.

"I've been wanting that for a long time," he said in a low voice. I smiled back at him, and a triumphant look came over his eyes.

"I enjoyed the kiss," I said. "But I don't want to get fired, Bruce. We have to stop. You're my boss."

"So you need to obey me," he said darkly, pressing his lips against my neck. His lower body was on top of mine, pinning me down, and I was helpless beneath him. I tried to squirm away but he growled softly in my ear, biting my earlobe gently in warning. "You know you want this, Jade."

He was completely right. But I couldn't admit it.

I craved his knot like nothing else at this moment. I wanted to be taken.

"Bruce, it's not right," I panted, feeling the heat from his heavy body on top of me. He was kissing my breast now, placing a trail of kisses on my nipple. He blew softly over my nipple, and the air made it stand straight up. Pebbling from desire.

*God, I was so horny.* My pussy was clenching endlessly, wanting to be filled badly.

"Shh, baby. Let me take care of you," he groaned against my breast, taking it into his mouth. He suckled on my breast, swirling his tongue around my nipple, and I gasped out loud. My pulse quickened with desire, and slick seeped from my pussy. "Mhmm."

I arched my back and moaned as he sucked my breast, spreading my legs underneath his body.

"I need you Bruce," I finally admitted.

"Good, because I need you too."

# Chapter 15

### Bruce

I craved her since the very beginning. And seeing her pussy spread on the couch earlier from the game was the last straw. My cock ached ever since.

Releasing Jade's wrists, I wrapped my fingers around her boobs, squeezing them together. Her breasts were so luscious and pink. I kept her legs spread with my knees as I knelt between them.

"Do you like it when I suck your big tits?" I asked her.

She looked at me with hooded lashes, desire in her eyes as she nodded shyly.

"I need you to give me an answer, baby," I said.

"Yes," she said, her lips swollen from our kiss. Bending, I pulled her second breast into my mouth, feeling her nipple slowly hardening under my tongue. The fullness of it in my mouth was indescribable. I hadn't been with a female in so long. To feel her soft round breast pressing in my mouth caused my dick to harden and swing in my boxers. Releasing her breast, I kissed her soft belly, squeezing her roundness and admiring her curves with my mouth. Every inch of her skin, I sucked and kissed.

"Do you want me to do that to your pussy?" I asked. I could smell her arousal. Her sweet scent overwhelmed the room begging for release.

If I touched her pussy now, I knew she would be wet with slick.

"Please, Bruce," she said. "Suck my pussy like that."

I would do anything for her.

Diving between her legs, I looked at her pink pussy spread for me. Open just for me. Little hairs were starting to grow on top and her folds, ruining Caleb's work. I didn't care, though.

I placed my hands on her thighs, spreading her legs apart further. I stared into her pussy, admiring how it clenched under my gaze. Her pussy would clench and release every second. She was aroused like nothing else. I had to give my baby relief. I wanted her pussy to clench around my tongue next.

"Your pussy is dripping on the sheets," I said.

"Are you going to clean it up?" she asked hoarsely.

"Oh, I will, little omega," I said as I ran my tongue against the top of her pussy. The taste of apple mixed with her musky scent was heaven. I was finally able to taste her. "My god, you taste so good, baby. You taste like apple cinnamon."

She moaned as I continued to lick her pussy in all the right spots. My tongue opened her up further as I went in deeper and deeper. I held the lips of her pussy open with my fingers as I rolled my tongue around her clitoris, which was starting to come out of hiding underneath her hood. Her clitoris pulsed underneath my tongue as I licked her there faster in short swipes up and down.

"More," she begged, widening her legs.

A lewd show that only I got to see. I pressed my tongue into her hole, and she gasped. I let out a growl as her pussy clenched tight around my tongue. She shivered as my growls caused her pussy to vibrate. She released slick as it seeped in copious amounts down her ass. I pulled my tongue away from her suctioning pussy as I quickly lapped up every drop of slick.

She tasted so sweet. Her honey on my tongue was something I didn't know I needed.

"Come for me, sweetie," I said, pressing my tongue harder against her clitoris as I swirled around and around. I wanted to fuck her with my dick but knotting her would be too much for her.

"No! I want your knot!" she screamed, squirming her little bottom away from my tongue.

"Oh, you're not getting away," I growled in her pussy when she dared to pull it away from my mouth. I dreamt of eating her out and languish between her thick thighs. "I'm going to say it again. Come for me so I can taste your slick."

"Please knot me," she begged, her pussy clenching, trying to get away from me.

I was relentless, though. I covered her engorged clitoris with my lips sucking her little bud like it was my last drink. She screamed and thrashed on the bed as she squirted a stream of slick. I continued to suck ardently, pressing my finger into her tight hole as I licked and sucked every inch of her trembling pussy. Her pussy clenched around my finger urgently as I lapped up every drop.

She was still trying to catch her breath while I feasted between her thighs.

Her liquid had spurted all over her thighs, and I happily cleaned her slick with my tongue.

"I didn't know you were a squirter, baby," I said, my voice muffled as I licked her inner thighs.

"It's embarrassing," she said, looking away.

I released her thighs and laid next to her. Her hair was fanned out all over the pillow, and her face pink after her orgasm.

"I love the fact that you squirt," I said. "It makes me feel satisfied that you're not faking when you come. I want to see you squirt whenever I go down on you."

"Oh," she said. "You don't think it's weird?"

"No, I love seeing your pussy gush with your slick. Don't ever be embarrassed."

She thought about that for a moment and reluctantly grinned. "Okay."

"You're thinking about something," I said. Jade was biting her lip which meant something was on her mind.

"Why didn't you knot inside me?"

"I didn't want you to regret it," I said. "At least this way, you're satisfied for a while since my pack riled you up sexually, and I get to taste you."

"Caleb is going to get so pissed," she said, looking worried as she laid a hand against my chest. Her soft hand on my chest triggered my cock, making it stiffen even more.

"We won't tell him," I said. "His loss."

Suddenly, Jade sat up and leaned over me. She grasped my hard dick in her little hands over my pants. I groaned in pleasure at how her fingers squeezed the right spots.

"I want you in my mouth," said Jade as she gazed at my hard cock with a twinkle in her eye. "I want to repay the favor."

"Are you sure, baby?" I asked. But while I was talking, she pulled my pants down my thighs. My cock was free and pointing straight up at her. When she grasped the length of it, I swore under my breath. "Squeeze the base some more, baby."

She leaned down and placed her mouth over the tip, slowly licking off my precum.

"Yum," she said like she was licking a popsicle. Her reaction made me even harder as I stared into her eyes while she took the length of me inside her mouth. She bobbed her head up and down while I watched her puppy eyes look innocently at me.

*Oh fuck.* I was going to cum so hard.

She then stopped, and I groaned as she released my cock from her mouth.

"Keep going, baby," I ordered. But she ignored me and sat on top of me instead. She lined up her pussy right on top of my cock and sat down. I groaned again as I felt my cock enter her tight warmth. Her tight hole welcoming my cock.

"Oh yes," she moaned, rocking back and forth on it. Her breasts swung up and down as she rode me like a wild woman. Fuck, she was determined to have my knot, and I was going to let her have it. She deserved it for how my fucking pack treated her. "Your dick is so big."

"You're so bad," I grunted as I grasped her hips, helping her bounce on my cock. "Clench your pussy."

She clenched her pussy tight around my dick, and I couldn't restrain myself. I exploded inside her, and she screamed as my dick swelled nicely inside her pussy, locking her to me.

"Fuck!" she screamed as my cock swelled even more. I knew she wasn't prepared for an older alpha's penis, but I wanted to satisfy her. "You're so big!"

She tried to pull off me as my cock swelled once more, but she yelled in pain.

"Don't," I said. "It'll hurt you if you try pulling away. Stay still, baby girl."

"I forgot about my heat suppressants," she moaned as she spread her legs further apart to ease the knotting in her pussy. "I might get pregnant."

"Hmm, I like the thought of your belly round with my child," I muttered, pushing my knot deeper into her, and she tried to pull away, gasping in pain. "You're hurting yourself, Jade. Please keep still."

I rubbed her ass as she lay on top of me, tears streaming down her face. I pressed my finger around her little asshole to help her stay stimulated while my knot tightened her to me.

"I don't know if I can get used to this," she said in a low voice. "Your knot is huge."

"Shh, it's because I'm older," I purred into her ear as I rubbed her anus in circles. I felt her asshole clench at my invading fingers, which meant she was getting stimulated again. "You wanted a thick knot to fill you up nicely, remember? You're the one who jumped on my cock, baby. I never told you to do that."

"You should have warned me," she whined.

"My dick is finished swelling inside your little pussy," I said. "It's done. Now relax while I play with your ass, okay?"

"Thank goodness," she exhaled as I kissed her tears away. She squirmed as I pressed my finger against her anus.

"Relax your bottom," I said. "I need to get you used to your future pack if Caleb resists taking you as our omega. They will take all your holes and I need to train you. I want you to be ready and prepared for their cocks."

"Okay," she said, compliant and laying on my chest still as I probed her bottom. I slid my finger inside her anus, and she yelped. "I never had anything inside there before."

"It's okay," I said to her. "I'll leave my finger resting inside your butt until my knot goes down."

Her anus clenched around my pinkie.

"This was fun," she said, kissing me on the lips and yawning. "It's so late, Bruce."

"I know, my dear," I said. "Sorry for keeping you up."

"Don't be sorry," she whispered, smiling as she leaned against my shoulder. I was happy I gave her the pleasure she needed after living in our pack house with four alphas. An omega's nature was to be dominated by her alphas, and we didn't give her that while we teased her.

"I don't want to leave you," I said, feeling upset that I needed to leave her here alone in this giant house. "Ever."

"I know, Bruce," she sighed as we kissed again. "I don't want you to go either. But I need this job."

"I'll come back tomorrow night," I promised. "I'll tuck you in every night like this."

# Chapter 16

### Jade

S tretching, I opened my eyes to the bright sun pouring into the room.

I noticed Bruce had disappeared from the bed, and the house was dead quiet. My entire body was sore from the brutal knotting of Bruce's. He had explained that as an alpha got older, their knots also got bigger. We talked about so many things late into the night that I could barely remember everything. I felt closer to him and I felt butterflies in my body, like I was glowing.

I grabbed my phone from the dresser and saw it was ten in the morning. Damn, it was so late.

Running to the bathroom, I showered and did all my morning essentials. I threw on a black pencil skirt and a purple shirt that was too small for me. I needed to go shopping for more clothes for sure when I got paid.

Walking into the kitchen, I pulled open all the cupboards and didn't see a single dish in sight. The fridge had nothing in it as well. It was the largest unfurnished kitchen I'd ever seen in my life. They must have just purchased this house. Leaning against the kitchen wall, I looked at my phone when I felt it vibrate. It was Keera texting me from the group chat.

**Are you ALIVE?** - Keera

I decided to answer them back. I hadn't talked to the girls in a while.

**I am** - me

**OMG we thought the matchmaker alpha pack kidnapped you** - Tiana

**So was it a scam? Are u even okay?** - Keera

**Ya, the pack I was matched with didn't like me. Then during the rainstorm, I couldn't leave their house** - me

**Omg, how did four alphas resist you?** - Tiana

**Or maybe they didn't...** - Keera

**They offered me a job designing their new mansion, so I'm living here for now** - me

**Umm, why** - Keera

**I got evicted** - me

The doorbell rang, and I hastily texted them as I made my way to the front door. I could see Dravin through the window carrying a shopping bag in one hand and a plate of food in the other. I opened the door.

"So this is where you've been hiding, huh?" he said in his thick voice. His voice was the deepest of all the alphas, and he was the most confident. He was bold with me, which made me nervous. I couldn't forget when he fingered me in the closet during our game last night.

"Hey, what's up?" I said, letting him in.

"I thought Caleb might have murdered you after last night," said Dravin, leaning against the door and looking at me.

"I didn't do anything wrong," I said indignantly. "Why does everyone think Caleb would punish me?"

"Walking out of his house like that," said Dravin shaking his head while chuckling. "Anyways, it's great to see you here and alive. I've brought you some breakfast."

He walked to the kitchen and set the grocery bag on the counter, pulling out loaves of bread and milk. He unwrapped the foil from the plate, and my stomach growled at the sight of the scrambled eggs and muffin.

I wanted to eat so bad.

But I hadn't surveyed the house yet at all. I was already behind on the project, and it was making me anxious.

"Thank you for the food, but I'll eat in a bit," I said, turning my camera on. "I need to take a few pictures of the living room first."

"I'm not leaving until you eat," said Dravin as he sat on the chair in the kitchen. I couldn't work with him here, distracting me.

"Alright, fine," I said, walking over to the kitchen island where the warm plate of eggs sat. Before I could grab a fork and take a bite, Dravin lifted me onto his lap, and I squealed. "What are you doing?!"

"I'll feed you, sweetheart," he said, hitching my skirt up around my knees. I could feel his hard cock straining against my ass as I struggled to get off him. "We're doing it my way, or else I'll stay here all day with you since I didn't get my fill."

I squirmed on his lap, getting turned on.

It didn't feel bad sitting on his lap. I felt his strong chest behind me as he swiveled the chair around to face the granite island.

"If you feed me, you'll leave?" I asked.

"Also, my finger misses your little pussy," he growled in my ear, and

I shivered. It was just like the time in the closet. My heart pounded faster as he lifted my skirt higher and higher around my thighs. "You're not wearing underwear?"

I gulped as I felt his fingers trail across my thigh, tracing the outline of my pussy.

"No," I said, holding my breath as his fingers spread my pussy lips apart. Then his thumb flicked my clit up and down until I trembled on his lap. My pussy came to life again on demand for each alpha who crossed my path in this home. I sighed and laid back against him, spreading my legs out on either side of his knee.

"Why aren't you wearing underwear? You wanted an alpha to have easy access to your little pussy, huh?" he said, pressing his middle finger deep into my channel. Spreading me with his thick finger. With his other hand, he scooped up a chunk of scrambled eggs with his fingers, bringing them to my mouth. "Eat up, little birdie."

I opened my mouth for his thick fingers as I got hornier. His fingers would go into my mouth as he fed me, forcing me to open my mouth wider each time. I didn't wear underwear because I was still sensitive from Bruce's knotting. I didn't think I could get horny again after that, but Dravin's fingers were arousing me once again.

His middle finger in my pussy lazily pumped in and out of me as my slick dripped onto his lap, soaking his jeans.

"Mhmm," I said after I finished the plate of scrambled eggs.

"I like feeding you," he said, wiggling the finger inside my pussy. "And I like fingering your pussy at the same time. How about if I stick a second finger inside you?"

"I don't think so," I said. "I don't want to orgasm all over your jeans."

"Why not?"

"I...I might squirt all over you," I muttered, looking down at the ground- wishing I could just hop off.

But his finger was pressed deep inside me, and his grip was strong as he held me still.

"Fuck yes. I want to see that," he said, quickly stuffing a second finger inside me, eliciting a moan from me as he stretched me out. He curved his fingers as he pumped in and out, hitting my sensitive region. "Squirt, baby. I'm not leaving this house until I can see that."

*Oh my god.* It felt so fucking good.

He fed me the muffin while he treated my pussy, and I willingly took that in my mouth while he praised me. The blueberry muffin was a delicious treat, but it was nothing compared to his fingers inside me. Even though my channel was sore, it felt good to have his fingers inside me, stretching me wonderfully again until I began to crave his knot.

Then he stuffed a third finger inside me, and I nearly choked on the muffin. His fingers thrust inside of me more aggressively this time, determined to force me to cum.

"Please, Dravin," I moaned. "It's going to be a big mess."

"I don't fucking care," he whispered in my ear, his hot breath making my heart pound hard. "I want you to squirt all over my jeans. I dare you to soak me in your squirt. I don't think you can, sweetheart. Do you feel my fingers desperate to feel your slick?"

"Stop, for real. I'm going to...I'm," I couldn't talk as I began to shake. I saw white as my pussy clenched, trembling around his fingers. Slick squirted everywhere, and I tried to close my legs to control it, but he lifted his knees, keeping my legs wide open. "Oh."

I rode the waves in a high as I moaned in his arms, letting my legs fall open farther to feel his fingers dig in deeper. I had squirted all over his jeans, no matter how hard I tried to stop it. Sometimes I could stop it, but it was too powerful this time compared to when he fingered me in the closet.

"Yes," said Dravin, rubbing my slick all over my pussy. He brought his fingers to my mouth, and I opened my mouth as I sucked my sweet slick off his fingers. "Good girl. You really can squirt."

I couldn't reply to him since his three fingers were still in my mouth. At that moment, I heard the front door open.

I tried to move Dravin's fingers away, but he stuffed them further into my mouth as he rolled the chair around to face the door. I struggled to move away, but the back of my head banged his chest, blocking me.

*Shit.*

Caleb got a good look at my spread pussy with Dravin's fingers in my mouth.

# Chapter 17

### Caleb

She looked so fucking delicious sitting there like that.

The omega looked helpless and annoyed as Dravin held her prisoner on her lap. Her exposed legs were juicy, and her little pink slit was open for me to see. I felt all the blood rush towards my cock, as it hardened.

I was shocked that Dravin managed to have her in this position with his three fingers in her mouth, her pussy dripping all over the floor. Maybe she did like to be submissive sometimes, even though she acted like she didn't need an alpha to handle her. She let out a muffled yell upon seeing me. She squirmed in his grip, her face red.

"Dravin, release her," I ordered, fed up with his games.

I was horny as fuck looking at her, but we needed to keep our hands off this omega.

"But she's so pretty," he grumbled, removing his fingers from her mouth, and she took in a big gasp of air.

She hopped off his lap and hastily covered her legs with her skirt, ruffled and visibly annoyed. She looked insanely adorable and I wanted to do nothing related to business. Every inch of my body was screaming to take this omega. She clearly enjoyed my pack.

A little too much.

"Sorry," she said in a high-pitched squeak.

"What's going on? Are you seducing my pack?" I asked. I enjoyed seeing her squirm, but I had to establish boundaries now, or else she wouldn't concentrate on her task, and it would be harder fighting the need to mate her.

"It was all his fault," she said, her eyes darting to Dravin. She blushed as she angrily crossed her arms.

My lips twitched, but I didn't smile. She needed to know how serious this was.

"We want to keep this arrangement professional," I said sternly. "Dravin, please leave. You're no longer allowed to be here alone with Jade."

"Yeah, yeah," he said, winking at Jade as he got off the chair.

Jade and I watched him leave out the door as he blew a kiss towards her. I observed Jade biting her lip, trying not to smile as he walked away. Fuck, she's forming connections to my alpha pack. He looked just as infatuated with her, judging from his smoldering last looks at her.

It would be tough to keep them separated.

"Alright, what ideas do you have for this living room?" I asked, walking around the empty space, trying to hide my erection. She made her way toward the living room, hurriedly taking pictures of the room with her phone.

"I'm sorry, I didn't get a head start on it yet, but I would like to go shopping to see what's there first," she said.

I was mildly disappointed that she was distracted by Dravin, but at least he fed her. I wanted to bang my head against the counter for forgetting her breakfast. It was a last-minute arrangement, so it slipped my brain. I would stock up this place with food so that she wouldn't starve.

"Let's go look around then," I said. "I have free time today."

"I have to warn you that I might take forever," she said, looking unsure of me accompanying her.

When we walked outside, she gasped upon seeing her car again in the driveway. I smiled, seeing her reaction.

"I took it to the wash," I said, looking at her little beat-up car, but it was shinier now. I wanted to badly get her a new car, but she would get offended. And it was the last thing I wanted to do.

She ran to it and put her hand on the hood in adoration.

"I missed my baby so much!" she said. "Thank you Caleb."

"You're welcome," I said, happy to see her so excited as she hopped into the driver's seat. I went around her car and sat beside her on the passenger side. Her eyes were closed as she leaned in towards the steering wheel, rubbing her nose on it.

"Sorry," she said, opening her eyes. "It just feels nice to have something of my own again. Getting evicted like that was hard on me. I felt like I was floating with nothing to support me. At least I can sleep in my car if I want to."

"I can understand," I said. "I built my own empire and started with nothing at first. I believe in you, Jade."

Startled, she looked at me. "You do?"

"You had the drive to become a nurse and lived on your own for so long, so I believe you could do whatever you set your mind to," I said as she started backing the car out of the driveway. "You'll become an amazing interior designer. I'm sure of it. What do you parents think about your dreams?"

I wondered why she was so reluctant to go back to them. I would do anything to have my father back.

"My parents provided a comfortable life for me. I feel bad for most omegas who had it bad, but I had a good foundation."

"Interesting," I said.

Jade rarely talked about herself, and I enjoyed listening to little tidbits of her life.

"I never drove an alpha in my car before," she said, looking at me sheepishly as she tried looking for the nearest furniture store around here.

"And I never had an omega drive me either," I said, surprised I didn't immediately get into the driver's seat and take over.

"Because you're too big and strong?" she teased and I laughed.

"I'd rather be the one to take care of my omega," I said.

"But I'm not your omega."

"Yeah, I got that," I said abruptly. The conversation always seemed to steer to this, and I didn't have an answer to give her. Maybe I was the one who was crazy. She liked my pack, and her gaze suggested she wouldn't mind if I rutted her senseless.

"What does the tattoo on your back mean?" she asked suddenly, and I was taken aback by her question. I was suddenly reminded of our hot night together on the roof of the party.

"My father passed away from an illness when I was a kid," I said. "He loved nature, and it represented that. It has his name in the middle."

"Oh, I'm sorry," she said. "At least you have your mom still."

117

"My mom...seems to be losing her mind," I explained. "I don't know what's happening to her. She says there's something following her. Like a ghost, and I don't believe in that stuff."

"That's so sad," she said, parking outside of a small furniture store. "Why don't you believe her?"

"Do *you* believe in ghosts?"

"Kind of," she said. "I wouldn't just disregard her completely. Pay more attention to her."

I thought about that. She could be right.

If my mother was telling the truth, she could be in great danger. But this was something that I wasn't ready to face yet.

### Jade

It sucked that I needed to be with Caleb for my first shopping trip on this big project. But he was adamant about accompanying me. I guess he was just as excited as I was for this project I was undertaking and wanted to be part of it.

As we looked around at the couches, Caleb didn't interfere when I looked at certain styles. But he couldn't resist giving his input on a few things. At times I imagined if this was how life would be if we were a mated pack.

"How about this couch?" he asked, sinking into a large black sectional sofa.

"It'll make the house too dark," I said, sitting on the other end.

"But it's comfortable."

It was indeed comfortable, but I needed to stick to my guns and not be pushed around. I was the designer, and I had a certain vision for the house.

"Yeah, I don't like it," I said. It didn't match my overall vision. A couple of beta females walked by us, staring at Caleb and giggling. My face heated, and I wasn't ready for the turmoil I faced inside me. I didn't like it, but I tried my best not to show that I was jealous. I didn't have a claim on Caleb in any way.

"Okay, how about that one?" he said, pointing to a beige couch. I immediately got up and walked over to it.

"It looks perfect," I breathed as I stared at the sectional. It was a nice sleek design that wasn't overwhelming and looked just as cozy as the first couch we saw.

"Good, looks like we're done here," he said, smiling at me. I realized we were standing too close to each other, so I pulled away, pretending to look at the couch some more. "I have to ask you something."

"Yes?"

"Have you been taking your heat suppressants? You seem more skittish around me lately," he observed as I moved far away from him.

"No," I said.

"Why not?"

"I lost them. The landlady must have taken them," I said, and it was way too expensive for me to get more. If I ever went into heat, I would probably just go to a heat center for omegas where alphas were waiting on demand to help me through a heat. An omega needed multiple mates to knot inside her to stave away the pain. If an omega went too long without mating while in heat, she could put herself at risk.

"We need to get you the suppressants right away," he said worriedly. "If you went into heat suddenly, it would activate my need to rut you.

119

You don't want that do you?"

"No," I said slowly, even though my body was screaming that it would be nice to have him deep inside me. I craved to be near him always and for him to be there with me. But it wasn't meant to be.

"You could be in preheat, and we don't even know it," he said, studying my face.

"I'm not," I said. I would probably know it right away, even though I've never actually been in heat. I was terrified of going into heat as an omega. All I heard was that omegas would be intensely horny during heat, wanting nothing but huge dicks inside her. And the only relief was when it knotted inside her. "I would know if I'm in heat."

He was quiet about it after that, and we went to the cashier to help us out with the purchase of the beautiful beige couch. They would deliver it the next day, and I was pretty excited about the first purchase.

But once we were back at the house, Caleb wasn't so sure about my heat.

He had a thermometer in his hand as I sat on my bed eating the pizza that he bought on our way back from our little shopping spree.

"Relax and take a slice," I told him, scooting the box of pizza towards him, which was sitting on the center of the bed. He glanced at it and licked his lips, but he was distracted by the thought of me being in possible preheat. "Listen, I'm not in pre-heat or anything. I promise."

"I can't take the chance of my pack impregnating you during your heat," he said. "After you're done with that slice of pizza- I need you to bend over for me."

# Chapter 18

**Caleb**

"*What?!*" she squeaked, her eyes wide.

"I need to take your temperature," I said, tapping the thermometer against my hand. It was the best way to determine if she was nearing her heat. "It needs to be done, Jade. I need to check every few days to make sure."

"I'm not doing it," she said adamantly, crossing her legs over the edge of the bed. She was so adorable when she thought she could fight me off.

"If a member of my pack impregnates you, you won't have a choice. You will be ours," I said. "Do you want me and my pack rutting you every night or not? It's your choice, sweetheart."

Her face reddened. She didn't have a choice now.

She quietly set her half-slice of pizza onto the box and wiped her hands on a napkin. I couldn't let her run around my pack while she was in heat. Her scent alone was powerful, and she was alluring in every way.

"Fine," she said, lifting her skirt and kneeling on the bed facing away

121

from me. Presenting her wide, luscious ass. "Just hurry up."

I almost faltered with lust as I gazed at her bouncy butt. I placed my palms on her soft cheeks, gently separating them. My dick stood straight up as I gazed at her pink pussy slit shining with slick. I rubbed the tip of the thermometer against her pussy lips, lubing it with her slick before placing it inside her ass hole.

"Relax your butt for me," I told her when her pussy clenched and her thighs quivered with anticipation.

"Oh, okay."

I spread her butt to take a good look at her anus.

I gently ran the tip of the metal thermometer around her sphincter to prepare her before I inserted it inside her dark, puckered hole. Her breathing grew louder as she pressed her butt towards me, arching her back like a cat in heat. Seeing her like that under my hands aroused every part of my being. Seeing an omega open and pliant like this was every alpha's dream. But instead of swiping my tongue all around her pussy or penetrating her with my cock, I slowly inserted the thermometer into her ass, and she let out a soft gasp.

"Good girl," I said, rubbing her ass cheeks gently as we waited for the thermometer to beep. I kept her cheeks closed to hold the thermometer still.

"Is it almost done?" she breathed.

I could smell her arousal.

The scent of apple hung thick in the air as I breathed in deep. I was so close to fucking her until she was worn out from my knot, but I had to calm my racing heart. I pushed my dick down with one hand, but it was hard as fuck.

*She's not mine.*

I stared at the numbers on the thermometer, willing it to hurry up. I didn't think it would be this hard to restrain myself from fucking this omega on my bed. I memorized every curve and the shape of her ass so I could take care of myself later when I was alone.

When the thermometer beeped, she was startled, and her butt jiggled. I spread her cheeks open and slowly removed the thermometer, which was wet with her slick.

"Hmm...you're not in preheat," I said, studying it as she twisted away and pulled her skirt back down over her panty-less privates. "But you're almost there, so you'll need to be careful."

"Thank god," she said, taking a sip of her soda. "Don't worry, I'll be careful. The last thing I want is to get rutted by you."

"Ouch," I said.

"You wouldn't be able to handle me," she said, winking.

"Trust me. You're dead wrong."

I sat next to her and grabbed a pizza slice, trying to cover my erection with my arm, but she had already got a good look when I was adjusting myself into a sitting position.

"You sound so confident," she giggled as she flirted unknowingly with me.

Fuck. I wanted to take her so badly. Right here. Right now.

*I can't.*

Damn it to hell.

"Tomorrow, I'll meet a new potential alpha pack for you," I said. "I'll tell them all about you, so by the time you go into heat- you'll have a pack ready."

"That sounds nice," she said sarcastically, while munching on her pizza and looking at me with her wide eyes and seductive dark eyelashes.

She looked hurt as she quietly munched on the food. My chest ached after telling her this information, but it was for the best.

## Jade

That night, I was lying in bed watching random cute videos on social media of cats being evil to their owners.

When Caleb left after lunch, I worked for a bit, looking around every room of the house and exploring this place. It was huge, but Caleb wanted me to focus mostly on the living room, sitting area, and dining room.

I secretly missed Caleb's presence and wondered if he felt the same or if he didn't care at all. There was a moment after he checked my temperature that I saw the look of feral lust in his eyes, and his erection in his pants proved it.

I heard the front door open, and I quickly sat up on the bed. A couple of heavy footsteps down the hall reminded me of Bruce's promise last night. That he'd be back tonight as well, and I smiled when he stepped into the room. But my eyes widened when I saw Nick trailing behind him.

"Nick! Bruce," I said happily. "You guys aren't supposed to be here."

"Hello darling," said Bruce, scrunching his nose. "Smells like pizza in here."

"Sorry, I know it's gross."

"Hey, hun," said Nick, removing his shoes. "I missed you."

"I missed you too," I said, aware that I was only wearing a thin red silk tank top with matching shorts under the bed sheets. "Caleb will fire me if he knows you're here."

My heart pounded in my chest.

Bruce was also removing his shoes.

"What are you guys doing?" I asked, finally.

"He won't mind if we all just cuddle for a little bit," said Bruce. "Do you mind if we cuddle you?"

"I don't, but are you sure?" I asked, wary of him. I was scared it would turn into a full blown-out menage between us if I let it happen. I couldn't control my omega urges to submit under an alpha.

"I just want to cuddle with you," said Nick. "Is that okay?"

"It makes no sense," I protested. "I'm not your omega."

"But you *will* be one day," said Bruce assuredly, settling underneath the sheets to my right while Nick went to my left. I was sandwiched between them on my back, and it felt so cozy with their strong hairy thighs pressed against my smooth ones.

"This is nice," Nick whispered in my ear, and my stomach clenched with desire.

"It's warm and toasty," I said, pressing my cold toes underneath their legs. One foot on either side, my legs a few inches apart.

"Did you miss me?" asked Bruce, softly touching my bare thighs as he leaned on his side. His wide, warm hand massaging my thighs did nothing to ease my arousal starting within me.

"I'm jealous you had sex with Bruce," said Nick, his hand rubbing up and down on my other thigh.

"It's not going to happen again," I gulped as I felt both alphas need to rut me. It was an energy in the air that I couldn't explain. I've never had so much male attention before, and I was enjoying every second of it even though it was wrong. So very wrong for me.

"You don't sound too certain," said Nick, kissing my shoulder.

"Please stop," I begged. "I don't want to be seduced by your alpha charms. Both of you."

Bruce chuckled, and Nick smiled against my shoulder.

"Don't worry, we won't," said Bruce. "We only wanted to say hi and cuddle you for a little bit."

"Liar," I said, turning onto my belly and hiding my face in the pillow. "You both came here wanting sex, knowing an omega was here and single. I'm not some object."

I realized it was a big mistake to turn onto my stomach because now their hands were on the back of my thighs, inching up to my butt.

"We're not here to take advantage of you," said Bruce, pressing his mouth to my ear as his hand cupped one of my ass cheeks. "But if you want pleasure, we're here to give it to you."

My pussy twitched, and arousal strummed through my body. I was aroused the minute they stepped into my bedroom. I was horny ever since Caleb took my temperature. I wanted to orgasm and I needed release badly.

"Okay," I whispered, and Nick immediately got to work pulling off my shorts. I tried to turn back around, but Bruce held me down by the small of my back to stay in place on my belly.

"This is a good position," he growled as his hand grasped my ass. "Stay like that on your tummy, baby girl. We want to explore your pussy and your ass."

I felt Nick's mouth on my left thigh and Bruce on my right thigh as they both worked their way up. Leaving a trail of soft bites and kisses on the back of my thighs. It felt like fire on my skin with every kiss and bite.

"Hey, you can't leave me out of this," said a deep male voice at the door.

My heart jumped in my throat as I tried to pull away, but Bruce held me down.

"It's okay, it's just Dravin," said Bruce. "How'd you know we were here?"

"You think I believed you? That you and Nick were going to the bar? When there is a real omega right here?" said Dravin indignantly.

I could hear Dravin unbuckling his belt, and I turned my head as Nick kissed the back of my thighs. Dravin threw his shirt on the ground, only wearing his boxers.

"Hey, big D," I said, and he laughed out loud, rushing towards the bed eagerly to me. Butterflies swirled in my belly at these alphas wanting me.

"You can lay on top of me, sweetie, while they play with you," said Dravin, pushing Nick out of the way and lifting me on top of him as we lay on the bed. His muscular frame underneath me was temptation itself, his cock already hard and ready. I was laying on top of him, my butt and thighs exposed to Nick and Bruce.

"Good idea," said Bruce.

*Things were getting out of hand now.*

But I wasn't complaining.

# *Chapter 19*

### Jade

D ravin captured my lips with his as Bruce and Nick pulled my underwear down over my legs.

"Mhm," said Dravin as I responded to his deepening kiss. His tongue pressed against my lips, going inside my mouth. Slick dampened my pussy as our tongues danced around each other. While we made out, I felt someone spread my legs around Dravin.

I gasped against Dravin's mouth when I felt a tongue circle around my pussy.

"Let me see her ass," said Nick, and I felt him spread my butt cheeks apart as he took a look. "Her little hole is blinking at me. I wonder if I can get her to slick from her anus."

"Oh," I sighed when I felt his hands massage my butt.

Dravin deepened the kiss even more, grasping my face and pulling me closer to him. His sideburns brushed my face, giving me tingles that radiated down to my core. He smelled of wood and palm trees, igniting my desire even more to have him.

I moaned as I felt Bruce's tongue swirling around my pussy, pressing into my core. Nick's little finger slid around my ass hole, even though I tried to squirm away. I was nervous when he was around there. I wasn't sure how freaky Nick was and what he was capable of. Dravin sucked the tip of my tongue while Bruce sucked on my clitoris at the same time.

"So good," Bruce muttered against my clenching pussy. "Release for me, baby. Give me a few drops."

Dravin's hands found my breasts, squeezing and pinching my nipples until they hardened. My muscles tensed, and my heart was pounding so fast. I could feel my clitoris swelling from Bruce's tongue. When Nick pressed around my sphincter faster and faster, I broke the kiss, moaning loudly into Dravin's muscular shoulder. Nick's finger pressing against my anus and Bruce sucking my clit, caused every muscle in my body to tense hard.

I couldn't hold it for long under their assault.

Slick shot out from both my pussy and my ass, even though I tried to hold it in. I've heard that omegas could release slick from their anus, but I never had it happen before until now. I collapsed against Dravin as he rubbed my neck and back with his big hands.

"Yes, that's beautiful," said Nick, plunging his finger into my ass. Then he removed his fingers, rubbing the slick around me.

"Told ya, she's a squirter," said Bruce as I felt their rough tongues licking every drop of my wetness. Nick's tongue whirled around my ass, pressing against every ridge and straining to go inside my hole.

Bruce's tongue was deep inside my pussy again, trying to suck any last drops from me.

"Oh my god," I said when I felt both of their tongues go inside my ass hole and my pussy. I felt self-conscious about not giving them pleasure while enjoying their touch and tongues on my body. I tried to pull my breast away from Dravin so I could go down his body and suck on his dick.

"It's okay," said Dravin as he sucked on my breast, his eyes rolling back in pleasure. "Let us have our fill. Tonight is all about *your* pleasure. Don't worry about us."

It was like he had read my mind.

Nick's tongue pumped in and out of my behind. It didn't hurt at all, but rather, it felt amazing. A deep pleasure that was unknown to me until now. He groaned and made growling sounds as he pushed in and out of my anus with his tongue.

Then he popped his tongue out after stretching out my ass.

"Are you sure you don't want me to knot you right in there?" asked Nick, tapping my tight anus.

"Caleb doesn't want me to have sex with you all," I said.

"Because you're almost in preheat," countered Nick. "He doesn't want you to get pregnant with our baby, even though we'd love for that to happen. You won't get pregnant with anal sex."

"That's true, but I'm a little scared," I gasped, enjoying the feeling of Bruce's sucking motion on my clit, taking me to new heights.

"You're made for my knot," said Nick. "We need to practice before you go into heat. Scream for me to stop, and I will."

Then I heard footsteps again at the doorway, and my heart nearly stopped.

Slowly turning, I saw Caleb standing there with a smirk on his face.

"Well, well, well," he said. "What do we have here?"

# Chapter 20

### Jade

"I'm sorry," I said, pushing Bruce's head away from my pussy.

I rolled off of Dravin and pulled the sheets up to cover myself. Caleb did *not* look happy standing there, but I could see his obvious erection at the sight of me being sucked to orgasm by his pack.

"I knew this would happen," said Caleb, shaking his head. "Guys, get off the bed."

At his command, Bruce, Dravin, and Nick got off the bed without a word, standing protectively around me. My chest swelled as they prevented me from seeing their angry pack leader.

"None of this is her fault," said Bruce. His voice was raspy from sucking on my pussy. "If anyone is going to be punished, it should be us."

"We're just having fun," said Dravin. "We're not going to knock her up."

"You're no longer allowed to come into this house anymore," said Caleb sharply. "Give me your keys. All of you. And she will be punished, so you will all learn a lesson too."

131

One by one, the men dropped their keys into Caleb's hand. My heart raced at what he had in store for me. I was scared to death but also remembered I could just leave this house and this monster of a boss I had. He didn't have a right to control my personal life, but apparently, he thought he did. I watched Caleb between the little space of Nick and Bruce's bodies blocking me off from him.

"Caleb, it's not her fault," said Nick, trying again as Caleb shoved his alphas out of the way to get to me. Caleb had a pouch hanging at his waist, and he dug his hand into it after giving me a stern look.

"You've all been coaxing her into heat," said Caleb.

"I swear that wasn't what we meant to do," argued Dravin. "We are all attracted to her, don't you see that?"

Caleb ignored him as he stalked toward me.

My palms were clammy, and I was shaking as I watched him. He pulled out a small switch that looked like a rubber spatula.

"You need a good spanking, don't you, little omega?"

"Please, don't," I said, backing away from him on the bed. The messy sheets clung around my ankles, but he grasped my ankle, pulling me onto his lap. My butt faced the air as I lay there face down on his lap.

I struggled to escape, but his grip was like metal, holding me still. Bruce shouted in protest, approaching me, but Caleb barked at him, stopping him in his tracks. I could feel Caleb's powerful alpha energy in full control of his pack.

"Either I fire you, or you'll get a spanking," he growled. "Pick one."

"It's not fair," I whined. "You already know I need this job desperately."

"You were reckless," he said. "You need to be taught a lesson. Can you imagine if my pack impregnated you?"

"Why don't you want me in your pack?" I shouted. "Am I *that* hideous?"

"Pick. One," he said again clearly without answering my question.

"I'll take the spanking," I whispered, shaking like a leaf in his grip. There was no way I was ready to walk away from this job. If I had to walk around with a sore butt tomorrow, so be it.

His hands caressed my bottom, and with every second, my heart pounded faster.

"You've been a bad girl seducing my pack every night, haven't you?" he asked. Then his palm came down with a loud smack on my right butt cheek, and I gasped quietly with the bedsheet stuffed around my mouth. My butt bounced at the impact, and he once again caressed my butt.

Then he smacked my left butt cheek.

"I didn't," I said, pulling the bed sheet out of my mouth to talk.

"Yes, you did," he said, now using the switch on me. I yelped as it came down hard on my ass. "I'm going to mark your sorry little ass so you can remember this. Then next time, you'll keep your legs closed around my pack."

I blinked back tears as I felt my ass burn and my pussy clench with arousal. He brought the paddle to my upper thighs, and I yelped again as it glanced off my pussy.

"Please, I'm sorry," I said.

He spanked me again, this time right in the middle. I clenched when my slick began to seep out. Even though my butt burned, I was getting horny.

"Nice and red," he finally said. "Do you promise not to spread your legs again with my pack?"

"Yes, I promise," I gasped as I felt his hand fondling my pussy. He ordered his pack to leave, and I heard the front door slam shut. I knew they were upset and angry at their leader, but Caleb could unleash even more of his fury if they said anything else.

"One last thing," he said, and I felt a cool metal press against my asshole. "I'm going to stick this plug into you so you can remember your punishment."

I tried to desperately get away, but it only served to make him hard underneath me. He twisted the plug into my opening, pressing it deep into my anus. I yelped as I felt myself being stretched back there. It didn't hurt since Nick had thankfully made me release slick from there and warmed me up nicely. It was a nice full feeling back there, but I didn't want Caleb to think I was enjoying it either.

Caleb inspected my ass, and I felt something cool as he squirted something onto my ass.

"It's a cooling cream," he said as he slowly rubbed my burning bottom. "It hurt me just as much as it hurt you. Please don't make me spank you again."

I felt my tears start to fall as I quietly cried into the bedsheets, my face away from him. I was shocked at myself. The tears came out of nowhere, and I didn't intend for it to happen. My tears of embarrassment soon turned to fury.

"Who do you think you are? This was so humiliating," I said through gritted teeth. I couldn't believe I let him do that to me. *Where the hell did my self-esteem go?* After everything my mother taught me, I let an alpha spank me. "My mom taught me better than this."

He let out a sigh.

"I needed my pack to see how serious I was," he said slowly. "You would also have had to face the consequences of pregnancy."

"Why? What's so bad about me hanging out with your pack?"

I was so confused. But I was determined to get to the bottom of this. I couldn't handle any more of his cryptic messages and his pushing me away from him.

"Because you might get hurt like my late wife," he said.

"What do you mean?" I asked. He wasn't making any sense.

"The Shadow Wolf," he said. "I'm worried it'll get you too, and I'll never be able to sleep again. I had nightmares for nights on end, reliving my late wife's death. I'm not prepared to endanger another omega just for being with me."

My fury soon began to dwindle when I saw how vulnerable he was being with me right now. He was finally opening up to me.

"I don't know what scratched me, but it had to be a coincidence," I said as I felt his hands gently rub the cooling cream all over my thighs. The burning stopped, but I still felt a mild uncomfortable sensation on my skin. "I'm willing to take the risk. I really like Nick, Bruce, and Dravin."

"I'm sorry," said Caleb. "It can't happen. It's impossible."

Then he gently lifted me off his lap, and I laid on my side, facing him with the plug still in my bottom. He stared into my face and carefully rolled my tears onto his thumb.

"I'll just do my job then," I said. "I don't want to see you either, except for work-related things."

"Not even as friends?"

"No," I said firmly. "If I'm around you, I would want you or your pack. It's hard for me to explain."

As I said the words, I felt sick to my stomach. But it was the only way.

He was pushing me away so hard I didn't have a choice. I needed to take care of myself, especially for my mental well-being.

"I'll respect your wishes," he said darkly. He didn't look happy at all, but I didn't care. I was still upset at him, too, that he dared spank me. "Sleep well, Jade. I'm sorry this had to happen."

"It's fine," I said, turning away from him.

I heard him leave the room, and I let out a big sigh.

I couldn't lay on my back because my butt burned, so I stayed on my side. Earlier tonight, I was so excited for Bruce to get here and now I felt deflated and defeated. All hope seemed to collapse out of me. Now I would focus on working hard without any distractions from the alphas. I looked at my phone when it lit up. It was Bruce, and I couldn't even smile like I usually did when I saw a text from him.

**I'm sorry, baby. Are u okay? I hope he wasn't too harsh** - Bruce

**I'm okay :/** - me

**I wish I could hug you and kiss you. But I don't want it to happen to u again** - Bruce

**I know** - me

**We'll figure out a way to be together. I promise, sweetie** - Bruce

I tucked my phone underneath my pillow so I didn't keep texting him. The more I texted and got attached, the worse this transition would be. I needed to distance myself, regardless of how anyone felt.

I needed to be strong and not let my omega instincts take over. I needed to focus on my career and my future.

# Chapter 21

### Jade

Over the next few days, I stayed true to my promise.

I didn't answer the door to any of the alphas, although once in a while, I'd see one of them stalking me from outside the window, mostly Dravin, to check on me.

Caleb would call to check on my progress but wasn't micromanaging everything like the last time. It was lonely, but the arrangement worked out fine. The house was slowly coming together as I stood in the living room watching the beta contractors hang a giant painting.

I was proud of the polka-dot painting I hunted down from a second-hand shop.

"Just a little to the left," I instructed. They moved the painting around until I was finally satisfied. I walked to the kitchen for a glass of water. I was pretty thirsty after directing the workers for hours this morning. As I sipped on the water, I leaned against the kitchen counter, staring at the time on the microwave. It was one in the afternoon already.

I nearly dropped my glass when I heard a loud shout coming from the living room.

Leaving my glass of water on the counter, I quickly ran toward the living room. The two contractors had gotten off their ladders and stared at each other in shock as if they'd seen a ghost.

"What happened?" I asked.

"Our ladders started shaking like crazy. I'm getting the hell out of here," said one of them, grabbing his ladder and making a beeline out of the front door.

"No, wait!" I shouted after him, wondering what the heck was going on. I turned back to the second worker, but he was also shaken up and ready to leave.

"This house is freaking haunted," said the other contractor shakily as he also grabbed his equipment. "Sorry, lady."

"What the fuck," I muttered to myself when I was alone in the house again. What was I going to do? They were supposed to help with hanging the curtains in the rooms next. I walked to my bedroom and grabbed my phone, dialing Caleb's number. My heart started to pound a little faster when I heard the phone ringing. I didn't want to call him, but he needed to know what was going on.

"Yes, Jade?" he answered on the third ring.

"The contractors left," I said and explained the entire story.

"I'm coming."

"No, that's not necessary," I started to say, and then I felt a small tug on the bottom of my jeans, and I screamed. When I looked down, there was nothing there.

"I'll be right over there," he said, hanging up when he heard me scream.

I hopped on the bed, scared of whatever was happening in the house. I've always felt like something was off in the house but I never felt a tugging on my clothes or anything like that before.

I hadn't seen Caleb ever since the spanking, and my heart was pounding hard in my chest at the thought of seeing him. I was wearing jeans with paint all over it and suddenly worried about how I looked.

Screw the damn ghosts. I quickly got off my bed and ran to my boxes. I didn't have time to organize anything, but I quickly sifted through several clothes until I could find something decent.

I changed into a pair of white leggings and a black low-cut shirt. It was the best I had for now. Looking in the mirror, I untied my ponytail and fluffed my long black hair around my shoulders. I looked okay, just a little plain, so I put on a little bit of makeup to enhance my eyes. I had no idea why I was panicking, but I didn't want to look terrible when he came over for the first time in days.

Within minutes, I heard the front door opening, and I took a deep breath before heading over to the living room.

"Jade," he said, his gaze raking over my body from head to toe-lingering on my breasts. My face warmed and I bit my lip.

To my alarm, Caleb looked like he hadn't slept in days.

His usually neat hair was mussed around his head, and he wore a gray shirt that looked like it needed to be washed. His black sweatpants hung loose around his waist like he couldn't care less about his appearance.

"Everything is fine now," I said hastily. "The contractors left, and I was just wondering if you could get us a couple of new workers."

"Are you okay? I heard you scream on the phone," he said, walking towards me- his eyes never leaving me.

I gulped.

"I'm okay," I said and thought to lie about it. "My clothes just got caught on something."

"Alright," he said slowly. Then he turned to see the work I'd done in the house. "Wow, with the couch, rug, and the painting. It all just comes together."

"Do you like it?" I asked hesitantly as he admired my handiwork.

"Very nice," he said, turning to me. "I can see what you can achieve without my pack distracting you."

"I'm glad you approve," I said, pleased that he liked it. Caleb pulled out a wad of cash from his pocket and handed it to me. "I can't accept that. You're already letting me stay here. I don't need all that."

"Take it," he said, and I quietly put it in the kitchen drawer without counting it. After he left, I'd count the money without feeling too guilty.

"Thanks," I said.

"Take a walk outside with me?" he suggested.

"Sure."

We walked towards the back of the house, past the double kitchens, as he held the doors open for me. When our arms brushed each other, I felt a flutter in my soul. The air was thick and heavy with tension. I wasn't sure if it was just my imagination or if he also felt the sexual tension.

It was a sunnier day today, instead of the gloomy rain we'd had for days. We walked along the cement pathway as it wound down between plants.

"Would make a beautiful garden one day," he said.

"I like walking out here to clear my mind sometimes," I said, inhaling the fresh air with the sun on my skin.

"Do you?" he asked, looking at me with bloodshot eyes.

"Yes. But how about you? You look like you haven't gotten any sleep."

He stopped walking, and I stopped alongside him.

"Because I couldn't sleep," he said slowly, his eyes on me. I could see his eyes darken as he stared at me. My heart beat faster, and I tried to take deep breaths to fight the impending desire. "I have been thinking about you."

Now my heart was literally thumping out of my chest. I had no idea what to think as my brain scrambled for something to say.

"Why? What's wrong?" I asked. I was filled with nervousness and concern for him but also scared of his answer.

He sighed and looked off in the distance, scrunching his eyebrows. I softly grasped his wrist, and he looked down at my hand, gripping his wrist, his nostrils flaring at my touch.

"Don't...I don't have much control around you," he sputtered. "*Fuck it.*"

Then he kissed me.

I couldn't believe it as his lips touched mine in greedy desire, ready to take what was his. I was too shocked to move as I allowed him to kiss me in the garden. He cradled the back of my head, adding pressure to the kiss. My eyes drifted closed as our kiss intensified and deepened. I absorbed the feeling of his muscular arms around me, his unshaven face rubbing against my face, and his unwashed musky alpha scent, causing fires of desire in my core.

When the kiss ended, I was breathless, and my face was hot.

"Oh my," I said, opening my eyes. He stared thoughtfully at me, his green eyes still dark with desire. It scared me, but I knew he was feeling it too. He craved to be around me too. Even without words, I knew.

"I couldn't handle the thought of never seeing you again," he said. "I want to be around you. I want to be in your presence at all times. Do you feel the same way, Jade?"

"Yes," I said softly. He traced my chin to my jawline with his finger. His touch ignited the fire within me. "I want to taste your lips again."

"Let's take this to the bedroom," he growled, lifting me high as I squealed and wrapped my legs tight around his waist.

I bounced on the bed as he dropped me onto it.

He crawled on top of me, kissing me on the lips again as his hands explored every inch of my body. My legs were still wrapped around his waist as he kissed me thoroughly. His hands squeezed my butt through my leggings.

"Let's get these damn leggings off. Watching you strut around in them was torture," he muttered over my lips, his hot breath sending chills down my spine. His darkened eyes were only intent on one thing. To take me. Even if I wanted to run away, his look showed me that he would hunt me to the ends of the earth for me. "I need to be inside you. Right. Now."

My fingers were shaking too much to pull my leggings off, so he took control. His fingers dug into my waistband, pulling my leggings and underwear down over my thighs. Before removing them, he knelt between my legs, staring at my panties and the dark stain on my white leggings.

"Don't look at that," I said, ashamed.

"You've wet your panties, little omega," he said, pulling them off as he studied them. I was naked now except for my black shirt. I quickly pulled my shirt over my head and flung it onto the floor. I wanted him completely. Knot and all. I was scared that if I disappointed him, I would never get to be his omega, and I would never see Dravin, Bruce, or Nick again.

I blushed as I watched Caleb sniff my panties.

"Why are you doing that?" I whispered.

"Alphas have a thing for scents," he growled, closing his eyes in pleasure as he sniffed the seat of my panties to his fill. "You slicked in your panties before I even got here. Were you excited that I was coming to see you?"

"Yes," I admitted, my face hot. Feeling like a total slut.

"I see," he said, dropping my panties onto the ground next to the bed. He pushed me down on the bed, and now I was on my back. He spread my knees apart and gazed at my pussy. My face heated, and I suddenly wished I had shaved earlier. He liked a clean-shaven pussy, but I never thought he'd be here today. He ran a finger down my hairs and in between the wet folds of my pussy. Then he inserted his finger into my throbbing core. "Do you want my knot inside here, sweetheart?"

143

# Chapter 22

**Jade**

"I do," I breathed.

His finger felt good inside my heated core, but his knot would be so much better.

Removing his finger from my pussy, his eyes roaming down at the length of my body. His gaze rested on my breasts. He grasped my breasts and dipped his head between my legs. His hot breath seared my pussy, making me tremble. His body was lean and hard as he nestled between my legs, using his chin to separate my thighs further apart.

"I love looking at your wet pink slit," he said, sticking his tongue out and resting it over my clit. He didn't move. He just let it sit there.

"Please," I said, trying to hump his tongue.

"I want to feel your clit pulsing on my tongue."

I groaned.

The longer he let his tongue rest over my clit, the more engorged and swollen my clit became. He didn't even have to do anything, and my arousal grew wilder by the second. I needed release badly. Ever since he stuck the toy in my bottom the other day, I tried to seek release with my fingers, but it wasn't the same as an alpha eating me out.

I needed release. And I needed it badly.

"Please don't tease me," I begged. I spread my legs farther apart to coax him to move his tongue. I arched my hips, but he growled, keeping my hips down on the bed.

"Your clit is pulsing very hard," he said, now moving his tongue around in circles.

I gripped the bed sheets, enjoying the way his tongue slid over the sensitive nerve endings around my clit. His tongue was dry in some places, pulling my clit further out of its hiding spot and almost making me cum all over him. I was about to climax.

"Please, harder!" I shouted.

He suddenly removed his tongue, and I felt bereft.

"Not yet."

"Why?!"

I wanted to scream with frustration. I quickly dipped my hand between my legs to finish the job, but he grabbed my hand, stopping me.

"You will cum on my dick," he said, pulling off his sweatpants and abandoning them on the end of the bed. He pressed the tip of his dick against my clit, holding it there for a few seconds. "Do you think you can squirt all over my cock, baby?"

My eyes widened. His pack had told him about my squirting.

*They were talking about me.*

"Yes," I whispered.

"Touch it first," he ordered, bringing my hand to it. I gripped his raging cock in my hand. It was thick and veiny as I slid my hand up and down, feeling him. I wondered if it would hurt. He was big, and I was suddenly scared it would hurt like Bruce's cock. I felt his hot liquid dribble a little. "I need to be inside you. Now."

Without another word, he plunged into my pussy, and my legs tightened around his waist. His cock stretched me wider and wider the deeper he pushed into me. Every inch of him elicited a moan from me. I was stretched to my limits before with Bruce, so thankfully, it didn't hurt this time around.

"Oh god, Caleb. It feels so good."

"Good," he said, his hungry bulge pounding into me. "Your moist center is squeezing my cock so hard. *Fuck*."

His hips moved with mine as I arched to meet him with every thrust.

His balls made slapping sounds against my sore ass, reminding me of his punishment.

"Oh yes," I moaned.

I was on the edge of the precipice. I was ready to cum all over his cock.

"Squirt all over my hungry dick," he groaned, pistoning into me. His thrusts were harder, faster, and nearly taking me off the bed. I felt like a rag doll as his cock raged inside of me, seeking release. My pussy couldn't clench anymore around his throbbing penis.

I screamed as I saw fireworks. My pussy clenched one last time, slick dripping down my ass. Flooding our union. He also came with a loud roar, slamming into me one last time, his cock lifting me off the bed.

"Oh, Caleb," I said, trembling underneath him as I rode down my powerful climax. He was breathing hard on top of me, trying to catch his breath as his cock knotted inside me.

"Fucking hot," he said huskily, kissing me on the lips. The kiss was sweet but still sensual as hell. I couldn't get enough of this alpha. When he pulled away, I felt the lingering imprint of his lips on mine.

"I agree," I said, relishing how his knot trapped his hot semen inside me. I reached around, feeling his cock and how it swelled around the base of it- the entire thing inside me. His over-heated alpha body resting over mine was delicious. I ran my fingers down his chest hairs, and he rolled to his side, facing me and gripping my hip.

"Your body is gorgeous," he said.

"Thank you," I said, my face heating as his hands roamed to my tummy.

"So luscious and plump."

"You don't think I'm too big?" I asked recklessly. But I wanted him to be truthful.

"You're just the perfect size. It's not only your body that's appealing, you know," Caleb said, tracing my face. "You have a beautiful soul."

I wanted to ask him the all-important question. But I kept clamping up at the thought of asking him if this meant I was his omega forever or not.

Maybe it was too early to ask.

He closed his eyes and laid his head against mine. Before I knew it, he was breathing softly, sound asleep.

I decided to let him bring that up if he really wanted me. Keera would probably kill me for wasting more time with him if he wasn't serious. She always wanted me to be more open in relationships and to let it blossom. Even though I *was* blunt at times, relationships were scary for me.

To be so vulnerable for my heart just to be crushed was terrifying.

"Wake up, little omega."

I slowly opened my eyes, wondering if I dreamt that we just had sex and knotted. When I saw Caleb next to me and the warmth of his body against mine, I smiled.

"Oh, you're still here," I said lamely. I had no idea what to say to this huge alpha who just knotted inside me. And he was watching me with those dark, lustful eyes of his.

"I am, but I have to get going in a few minutes," he said, looking towards the window. It was sunset outside, and I realized we slept in each other's arms for a couple of hours at most. "Do you mind if I use your shower?"

"Of course not! It's your house."

"This is your space, though, and I will respect that," he said, getting off the bed and heading into the bathroom. I heard the water turn on. Flopping over, I saw the light from his cell phone still on the dresser.

I wanted to take a peek at his phone.

*No, stay away from that. He's not even your alpha.*

Against my better judgment, I quickly grabbed his phone just to see what type of alpha he was.

God, he would be so pissed off at me if he knew.

My breathing quickened as I opened his text messages.

I scrolled down his text messages and stopped when I saw my name. He was messaging some random guy about me. My mouth dropped open when I saw he was arranging a meet-up between me and an alpha pack on Friday.

*What? He was still matchmaking me off for his money.*

When I heard the water turn off, I carefully placed his phone where it was just as I found it. The texts were enough to make me boil inside. Why did he have sex with me if he wasn't serious? I thought Bruce had knocked some sense into him. Well, I secretly hoped that was the case. But it clearly wasn't.

He wanted to use me before he sent me off with a new pack.

Typical.

I kept a neutral face when he returned to the bedroom with all his muscular nudeness. He was a sight to behold with a white towel around his waist, his dark hairs disappearing down to his naval. But I didn't care anymore.

"What's wrong?" he asked when he caught me staring at him as he pulled on his clothes.

"Nothing," I said, quickly looking away. I didn't want to say anything to him right now. He would know I went through his phone, and he wouldn't be exactly pleased with what I did.

After putting on the rest of his clothes, he walked over to me on the bed and kissed me again.

"I can't wait to see you tomorrow, babe," he said.

In my head, I was screaming. *What was he playing at?!*

"Yep, me too," I replied, poker-faced.

"Are you sure everything's okay?" he asked again, studying my face.

"For sure," I said as cheerily as possible.

Once he left the house, I got off the bed- angrily throwing the covers off me. I've never felt so humiliated in my life. He never mentioned me being in his pack or being his omega. It was completely outrageous that he'd do a test drive on me before matching me up.

In the shower, I tried to scrub my skin as much as possible and between my legs to erase any memories of his touch. My chest ached, and I had to keep reminding myself that he wasn't mine.

He was never mine. I'd never see his pack again.

Tears welled in my eyes, and I just let it flow as I rinsed my body. My throat was tight as I took deep breaths, trying to restore peace in my soul. The hardest part was that his pack genuinely wanted to be there for me. They came to cuddle me and make me feel safe. And for that, they were punished by watching *me* get punished. The tears came down harder as I held a fist over my heart.

I couldn't handle the memories any longer.

Some part of me told me I would never find my true pack who would love me. A pack who was honest and cared about me. I stood under the shower allowing the water to wash over me as I shuddered against the wall, my shoulder aching from the hard surface.

After my shower, I got dressed and began throwing all my things back into the boxes. I couldn't stay in this house anymore. It was too painful, and Caleb wasn't serious about me at all. I wanted Dravin, Bruce and Nick but I couldn't have them.

When I finished packing, I wrote a letter and left it on the kitchen counter. I remembered the money he paid me, and I pulled it out of the drawer, counting out the three thousand dollars. It was enough to survive off for a couple of months at least. Then, grabbing one box at a time, I stuffed them into the backseat of my car. Once the last box was loaded in, I looked back at the house one last time.

Wiping my eyes, I started driving to my parent's house.

# Chapter 23

### Caleb

"What time is the meeting with the omega set?" asked the alpha over the phone.

*Fuck.*

I was so fucking tired of these alphas being so pushy about their potential mates. I didn't get enough time to find a replacement omega for him, but he thought he was getting Jade. *The hell he will.*

The following day, I was driving to the new house, excited to see Jade again. Of course, we'd talk about business first, then fuck later. My dick twitched in my pants, coming to life as I remembered her incredible ass and thick juicy thighs. I wasn't ready to tell my pack, as I didn't want to share her just yet, but I was sure they could smell her scent on me.

"The omega canceled again," I said hastily. "Don't worry, I'll find you a new one."

"You promised Jade to us," he said, his voice lowering. "Do I detect something fishy going on?"

The truth was that I matched her to them after her little punishment. I was hellbent on getting her matched up, but I regretted it soon after I called Tim's pack. After the phone call, I couldn't shower or do anything normal for days until I saw Jade again.

She was my life now. She was *my mate.*

"Nothing fishy is happening," I said. "If you don't trust my company, there's no use doing business with me."

"I trust you'll get through to Jade and convince her to meet us," said Tim. "Didn't you say she signed up to be matched too? So why is she canceling?"

"It's tough to snag an omega these days, brother," I said pacifying him for now. "I'll do everything in my power to either get her to reply to me, or I'll match you up with a new omega similar to her in description."

To me, no other omega compared to Jade. None at all.

"Fine, I'll follow up in a few days time," said Tim, hanging up on me.

*Asshole.* Yeah, he was definitely unhappy.

I parked the car in the driveway, noticing her car was gone. *Why would she have gone shopping already without me?* I thought she was excited to see me this morning too. Going into the house, I looked around. She left the house clean and tidy. Noticing a piece of paper on the kitchen counter, I picked it up. It was a letter from her.

*Dear Caleb,*

*This may seem random and sudden- but I'm writing to let you know that I no longer wish to work on the house with you. I appreciate you giving me a place to stay during the hardest time of my life. Say goodbye to Dravin, Bruce, and Nick for me. After last night, I realized I want something more serious, not just one-night stands with you anymore.*

*Anyways good luck in your search for your true mate.*
*Thank you for the opportunity,*
*Jade*

As I read the letter, my chest tightened with every word.

I crumpled up the letter and threw it in the trash. *She wasn't serious, was she*?! Why the fuck would she think it was a one-night stand? I dialed her number into my phone. I needed to talk to her.

What we had last night was as real as could be.

The phone rang and rang. My pulse pounded as I waited for her to pick up.

"Damn it!" I shouted as it went to voice mail. Then, in a calmer tone, "I don't know what kind of game you're playing, Jade, but it's enough now. Please come back, and let's talk about this."

*Did she not feel the connection we had from the start?*

I stomped towards her bedroom and saw that she had taken all her boxes. She wasn't playing around. She was serious. The sight of the bare room made me feel physically sick. I sat on the bed, inhaling the last of her scent in the air. My eyes burned with unshed tears as I looked around. I started replaying everything in my mind and what I'd done to make her leave. Did she want a formal pledge from me? I thought it would scare her if things moved too fast. I wanted her to be my pack's omega, and now she'd completely lost trust in me.

I punched the mattress, completely and utterly upset with myself.

Back at my old house, I was sitting in the living room with my pack-after gathering them for an impromptu meeting.

"What's up, Cal?" asked Dravin, sipping his beer, eyes on the television.

My pack was disgruntled with me ever since I spanked Jade in front of them. Bruce hadn't spoken to me in days, only for business-related things for *Enchanted Nests*. Nick was being Nick. He was in his own world of trying to expand our business. He threw himself into the work. No one spoke about Jade around me.

They sat around me, Bruce with his arms crossed, staring at me expectantly. Nick looked impatient, ready to run out of the living room and back into his office.

"It's about Jade," I said. Soon as I said her name, Bruce sat up a little straighter, Nick's eyes lit up, and Dravin set his glass of beer down on the coffee table.

"What about her?" asked Nick.

"Well I..."

"Get to the point, Caleb," Bruce grunted. I felt like he had the least patience with me.

"I slept with her yesterday," I admitted, my jaw tensing.

"Did you fuck her? Like sleep, *sleep* with her?" asked Dravin, his voice a rolling thunder. He would be intimidating to any other pack but not to me.

"I did," I said. I could sense the spirits of the alphas lifting in the room. They were hoping something would come of this. I hated to burst their bubble. "But she left today, leaving a note behind for me. She quit, and she said bye to all of you."

"Wait, that doesn't make sense," said Bruce. He could smell bullshit a mile away. "What did you do, Caleb? The whole truth."

"Nothing at all," I said. "After I took a shower and came back, she seemed a little bit weird to me, and then I came in today and found her gone."

"Did you make any commitment to her? That she would be ours?" asked Bruce, digging deeper.

I exhaled, gripping the sofa's armrest until it ripped.

"I did not."

"There you go," said Nick, shaking his head. "Why did you fucking sleep with her? Were you even serious?"

"I was dead serious," I said. "I was waiting for the right time to bring her back to you guys."

"Whatever, man," said Dravin, getting up, beer in hand.

"Wait," I said. "We need to find out where her parents live. That's the only place she could be staying at now."

"What will you do once you find her?" asked Nick. He was a 'take-action' sort of alpha.

"I'm going to ask her to be our omega."

"It's not going to be that easy," said Bruce.

"*We* will go down on our knees if we have to. She's mine," I growled.

"Ours," Dravin corrected.

Bruce pumped his fist into the air, and Nick's serious face cracked into the first smile I'd seen in a while.

"Exactly. And I'll be damned if another pack mates and marks her," I said. "Nick, please work on finding a new omega for the Hawthane Pack. There's no way in hell I'm handing Jade over to them. Bruce and Dravin, we need to find our omega as soon as possible."

"I'll get to work immediately," said Nick, dashing off to his office.

"We'll find her," said Bruce. "And hope to god, she'll want to give us another chance."

# Chapter 24

### Jade

*"What happened, Jade?"*

*"Are you coming back to us?"*

*"What happened to your job?"*

I was pelted with questions as I carried a box from the car into my parent's home. Unfortunately, they were all at home at this hour, and there was no sneaking in as I hoped.

"I'll explain. Just hold on," I sighed as I dropped the box into my old childhood room. The house was modest. It wasn't as ginormous as Caleb's new mansion, but it was enough for a smaller family like ours. Since my brother Jack moved out, we had a lot more space.

I walked past my three dads staring at me in the living room and my mom who was holding a pencil in her hand as she held her student's papers in her other hand. It was nightfall as I returned to my car for the second box in the trunk. As I made my way back, I tripped and fell onto the cracked sidewalk.

Fuck my life.

"Be careful, kiddo," said Dad Jon, reaching a hand out. I grasped it, groaning from the pain in my ankle.

"Shit, I think I twisted my ankle," I said, limping and hopping as he slowly walked me to the house. My other two dads, Seth and Rob, were at my car, carrying my boxes for me into the house.

"Hey, hey, no cussing," Jon chastised.

"Dad, I'm old as fuck."

"Jade!" he said, eyes round. "Then you're not too old to be grounded, young lady."

"I'm just joking, Dad," I said, wincing as he sat me on the couch. I reached down, massaging my ankle. My mother ran into the living room with an ice pack, applying it on my ankle. "Thanks, Mom."

"Doesn't look sprained," she said, pressing the coldness against my skin. It eased the pain immensely. I applied pressure on my foot, and I winced again. "Don't overexert yourself for a few days."

"I know, Mom," I said, without reminding her that I was a nurse.

After my dads brought my boxes into the two-story home, they sat around me in the family room expectantly waiting for me to explain what was going on and why I was moving back in with them. I was lying on the couch with my feet on my mom's lap as she held the ice pack to my ankle.

"Time to tell us what's going on," said Dad Seth, clasping his hands on his lap.

I sighed.

There was no more hiding it. I didn't care anymore at this point.

"Well, I quit my job," I said. Without waiting a beat, I told them the second shocking news. "And I got evicted from my apartment."

"What?!" said Rob.

I was mostly scared about my mother's reaction. After everything she drilled into me about being in a professional field as an omega, I knew she was angry. She was quiet. Worryingly quiet.

"I couldn't keep working there," I said. "Our boss is a freaking tyrant, and I'm just drained."

"How could you do this after everything?" my mom finally asked. "After all your schooling. We can help you get your position back with the Omega Rights Association."

"No," I snapped. I didn't want to stay and continue this conversation. I gingerly stood on my bad foot and grabbed a chair for balance. "I don't want to talk about this anymore."

"We love you," said Dad Jon. "Your mother only wants what's best for you."

"She's just scared her friends will hear about this. Her failure of a daughter," I said and looked over at Mom. Her lips were pursed, and she didn't say another word to me. I grabbed the ice pack from the couch and limped to my room.

⚜

Over the next few days, I was literally holed up in my bedroom.

I didn't want to get out for anything. My fathers would call me for hot chocolate and movies, but I would still not come out. I only left my room in the middle of the night to grab food without anyone there. I was lying in bed right now, staring at my phone. I hated leaving my room, especially when my mother was out there. She hounded me constantly of why I wasn't being productive.

Regardless of how Caleb treated me, thoughts of him and his pack flooded my mind constantly. There were a hundred voicemails from them on my phone which I didn't dare check. A constant ache in my heart and my soul that nothing could soothe. I'd wake up crying and mumbling without realizing it. I didn't want to talk to anyone. Not even Keera or any of my friends. That would require a lot of energy that I just didn't have.

But I knew I couldn't keep going on like this forever.

So when I saw the text from my cousin, Shanna, on my phone- I lit up a little. She wanted to go dress shopping for her wedding, which was apparently not canceled anymore but delayed to next year. I agreed to go shopping with her and a couple of her friends later today after she said I had great taste. It would have been evil of me to refuse.

As I worked up the energy to get off the bed and into the shower, I tried not to think of Caleb and his pack. I couldn't let my thoughts go there. It was the only way I'd be productive today. Heartbreak was real for me now on a whole other level.

"That dress is the one," I breathed as I gazed upon my cousin walking out of the dressing room. Her two friends gasped upon seeing her in her strapless dress covered in rhinestones. My cousin was a beta, and she was marrying a beta guy who she's been madly in love with since high school.

"So beautiful, Shanna," gasped her friend.

"Do you think so?" she asked, looking into the tall mirror, her face glowing. She was so lucky to be a beta and not have to worry about the heats that omegas went through. The only thing that sucked for her was that she was only with one guy. Betas were normally envious of the fact that omegas had two mates or more to get through heats.

"It's stunning. For real," I said. "Do you like it, Shanna?"

"I'll go with this one," she said happily, twirling in the mirror as she looked at herself. She had refused too many dresses, so we breathed a sigh of relief at the same time. "I love it."

Shanna bought the dress, and as she was getting sized for it- she wanted to know about what was going on in my trainwreck life.

"Nothing much," I said. "Just been busy at work, that's all."

"You look sad, though, and you haven't been talking as much," said Shanna as the shop owner measured her arms next. "Your normally bubbly self- deflated or something. I can't explain it."

"Well, I met an alpha pack," I said, deciding just to tell her and her friends. "The alpha leader wasn't serious about me, and I slept with him."

"So?" asked Shanna. "Doesn't that happen all the time?"

"She caught feelings for him..." said one of her friends who was more astute than her.

"I did," I said.

"Did you tell him how you feel?"

"A few times before, yeah," I said.

"If they hadn't fought for you, then they're not meant for you," said Shanna. "I suggest getting on with a new pack."

"You're probably right," I said, determined to let it go once and for all. I couldn't keep torturing myself over the fact that Caleb didn't want me. As I drove to my parent's home, I started feeling better after I had talked to my cousin and her friends. They were right. I could continue painting and doing all the things I loved to do. If all else fails,

I'll apply for another nurse position at a different clinic.

When I got to my parent's house, I was in for a major surprise when I got inside.

Caleb, Dravin, Nick, and Bruce were all in the living room talking to my parents. I couldn't back out and run since they'd all seen me already. I wanted to sink into the ground and die for not seeing their truck on the side of the road.

I was so stupid.

"What the hell are you all doing here?!" I said.

# Chapter 25

### Jade

"Jade, I want to know why you left," said Caleb in a low voice.

"Nothing, I was burnt out from the job," I said, my keys burning into my palm from how hard I was gripping them.

My parents looked perplexed seeing all four alphas in the living room for me.

"Is this why you quit your job?" my mom asked me- looking back and forth between us. I shook my head. At this moment, I really wanted to die. I wanted to keep the secret between Caleb's pack and me a secret to the grave, but everything was out in the open now. "Is this why you've been crying all night? I thought I taught you better than that daughter."

*Fuck my life.*

"You've been crying?" Dravin turned to me. The familiar warmth in his eyes made me want to break down in tears.

"No," I said briskly. "Can you all please leave? Everything's over between us."

"No, it's not," said Caleb, stepping towards me until he was in front of me. He lifted my chin with his finger. "Did any of it mean anything to you?"

"It did until I saw your phone," I said, gritting my teeth. He was forcing me to say it. I didn't want to show that the texts hurt me.

"What did you see?" he pressed. His finger on my chin seemed to burn through my skin as I stood there, trying not to let the tears fall. His nearness had my heart thumping uncontrollably in my chest.

"You were arranging for another alpha pack to have me after we slept together," I said.

I heard my mother gasp.

*Damn it.* I forgot she was there.

Caleb looked surprised, and the rest of his pack glared at him.

"Get the fuck out of our home. You hurt our daughter," said Rob, his beard shivering with his rage.

I didn't stop my dads from pushing all the alphas out of the door.

"I can explain," growled Caleb as Rob wrestled him to the door. They were like giants in the living room, knocking over furniture. I knew Caleb could put up a better fight, but he wouldn't ever get my father's blessing if he hurt my dad.

"Don't you dare growl at me, pup," roared Rob, shoving Caleb out the door.

Rob shut the door after the pack left, and all my dads were staring at me with their arms crossed.

"Why did an alpha pack show up at our door?" asked Seth.

"You have some explaining to do," said Mom.

"It wasn't anything serious," I said. "I had a fling, and that's all. If you don't mind, I'm tired."

Ignoring their protests about leaving them mid-conversation, I headed to my room. My chest was physically aching, and I felt sick to my stomach. Seeing my fathers push the alphas I loved out the door hurt me. *Wait...I loved them.* Maybe I was just delusional, but the feelings had crept in over the time I stayed with them during the rainstorm. I couldn't deny my feelings for them, but I needed to bury it.

I heard two soft knocks at the door.

*Ugh.*

"Yes?"

"It's me. May I come in?" said Mom.

"Yeah," I said, even though I wasn't ready to talk. Like at all. With my head on the pillow, I watched her as she sat on the end of my bed.

"Do you still have feelings for that pack?" she asked.

"I don't know."

"As a mother, I don't like to hear you cry every night."

"Well, I'm not."

"Don't lie Jade sweetheart," said Mom, resting her hand on my ankle. I didn't trust her. Sometimes she'd act all concerned as a ploy to get me to talk. "I think you should follow your heart."

"What are you talking about?"

"It doesn't matter about your job anymore. You already quit," she said. "A job or career isn't everything in life. If you think this is the alpha pack of your heart, maybe you should explore it."

*Was this even my real mom talking?* I sat up in bed, resting my back against the headboard.

"But you always said..."

"I know what I said," she whispered. "When I was your age, I missed the opportunity to be with the pack I truly desired. I fell in love and thought the smart thing to do was stop it immediately to pursue my career. I never followed my heart. Don't get me wrong- I love your fathers, but an omega's power is also knowing who her true pack is."

This was the first time she ever opened up about her past relationships. I could feel the pain radiate from her body, and she looked towards the closed door furtively, hoping my dads didn't hear her.

"I didn't know," I said. "I'm sorry, Mom."

"Don't be. I'm happy now, but not as much as I would be if I just listened to my soul," she said, her fingers tightening around my ankle. "Do it, Jadey. I will support you a million percent. Follow your heart, and don't let anyone stop you. If the pack came looking for you, it should tell you something. And that Caleb guy...he's not horrible-looking either." She winked, and I smacked her hand away, laughing.

"Thanks, Mom," I said. "But what if they're just using me?"

"A pack obsessed with you will not. I don't believe for a second he would be willing to give you up easily."

When she left the room, I laid there for a few moments, pondering over what she'd said. I pulled my phone out and started listening to the hundreds of voicemails that Caleb, Dravin, Bruce, and Nick had left me.

*"Where are you, Jade? Why are you playing games with me?"*

*"I don't know what I did wrong. If you are listening to this, Jade, please come home. The house feels empty as fuck without you, babe."*

Tears streamed down my cheeks as I listened to each voicemail. My heart ached more and more with each one. The voicemails were frantic at first and then into sad acceptance. I didn't want to be apart from them either.

I decided I needed to go visit them tomorrow for closure.

I had to know.

The next day, I parked my car a few streets down, away from the alpha's old house. I needed time to think before I got there. I undid my seat belt and stepped out of the car, my heart beating in anticipation. I hoped I wouldn't run into any of them right now.

I had to gather my thoughts. To figure out my life because I had no idea what I was going to say to them.

As I walked towards the home, I freaked out several times, ready to turn back. I straightened my black sweater and adjusted the hoodie over my messy ponytail. It wasn't raining anymore, but there was a small drizzle. I had on jeans and black sneakers. I wasn't exactly dressed to impress today. I wanted to get down to business without them getting distracted by my boobs. I wondered if it would be awkward to say hi and stroll in.

I rehearsed what I would say several times in my head.

*Hey guys, so I just wanted some closure, you know? So that we can both move forward in our lives.*

It sounded okay but also lame in my head. I wanted to hear what Caleb had to say about the text and if they were really serious about matching me up with a pack for their *Enchanted Nests* business. I was a viable single omega, after all.

When I reached the driveway, sweat beaded down my back. Something stopped me as I passed by the guest house. An older woman with gray dreadlocks, a torn white dress, and a frail-looking body stared at me as she stood outside the house. *Was this Caleb's mother?* I couldn't believe how she was kept in such a dreadful state. She waved me down as I approached her.

"Hi," I said.

"You're the omega that my son is infatuated with," she said, her voice raspy.

"I wouldn't say he's *infatuated*," I replied, rolling my eyes.

"Please have tea with me," she said. "I would like to have some company."

"I don't really have much time," I said, hedging away, but she grasped my wrist. The smell of rotten meat emanating from her body made me want to vomit. But I felt sorry for this old lady. No one was taking care of her, and a spark of fury went through me at the treatment of her.

"Please, just for a few moments. I'm very lonely at times," she said. "And I'd love to meet the love of my son's life."

"Alright," I said, walking alongside her to the guesthouse. Her words made me a little more hopeful, but I was still wary. "What makes you think I'm the love of his life?"

"I know things, young lady," she cackled as we walked inside. "Let go to this room, here. Shall we?"

I followed her into the second room and was alarmed to see no sunlight shining into it. I walked further inside and gasped when I saw a large drawing on the ground written in red chalk. It looked like a picture of a pentagram. I knew that wasn't a good sign. When I turned back to look at her, she had disappeared from the room and had shut the door.

"Excuse me?" I said, walking to the door and turning the door handle. It was locked. "Listen, lady. This isn't funny. Let me out."

"Hold on, I'm just making tea for us," she said from the other side of the door, breathing hard. Why was she acting like this? She must have really lost her mind, and I began feeling sorrier for Caleb. I couldn't imagine this happening to my parents at all, and I began to appreciate what I had.

I heard scratching sounds on the wall behind me, and I quickly spun around. If there were mice in here, I was going to scream.

But something far worse was happening.

A pool of shadow was forming on top of the pentagram sign on the ground. Heart racing, I tried to turn the doorknob frantically with one hand while my back was pressed to the door.

"Please open the door!" I shouted. I watched as the pool of shadow began to take shape into a tall human-shaped body. The face and body of a large male appeared before me.

He wore a large black hooded robe, and his face was littered with scars. His red eyes landed on me, and his thin lips twisted into a wide smile.

# Chapter 26

**Jade**

I couldn't move. I was frozen in fear.

"Who are you?" I squeaked.

"You might know me as the *Shadow Wolf*," he said. "The king of all demons. My name's Argon."

My pulse was racing as I stood there dumbfounded. My eyes were glued to his red demon eyes. A scream stuck in my throat.

"Please let me out of here," I said. I tried to shout the words so Caleb's mother could hear me, but my voice was small from fear.

"Oh, that won't be happening, naughty omega," he rasped, slowly walking over to me.

I couldn't move any farther from him. My back was already up against the door, and there wasn't any space in this tiny hellish room. He stopped before me, and I could feel his fiery breath on my face as he breathed through his flaring nostrils. He smelled of smoke and dust.

"I didn't do anything to you," I said, cowering against the door. He reached up to touch my shoulder, and warmth spread from his fingers to my skin. The contact sent a frenzy of desire to swirl in my belly.

*No, no, no.* He was bad. He was the devil himself.

I steeled myself against it, clenching my thighs together.

"Every omega is mine," he said with that permanent smile. "But this time, I'll keep you instead of disposing of you afterward."

"Why are you doing this?"

"Zaneesha knows she shouldn't have played with dark magic. She wanted to restore peace through me," he said, rubbing my shoulder. The heat of skin through my sweater continually sent shivers down my spine. "She knew it would come with a cost. Over the years, my appetite was sated with omega sacrifices in the cave, but when that omega princess cast me out of that poor boy's body, I had nowhere to go."

"Why are you here then?"

"I tormented Zaneesha," he said, his smile getting even wider as he gazed at the door as if staring at our host directly. I heard her whimper on the other side of the door, and I knew she was listening to our conversation. "I tormented her until she gave in and conjured me up in this form using a dead alpha's body. And I would be promised an omega."

"Why don't you just go out and find your own mate?" I said. I was angry and confused. I flinched when his hand roamed to my neck, lightly squeezing it.

"I'm trapped here with the pentagram until Zaneesha can set me free," he said. "I'm going to bring you to heat, mate, and then mark you."

"Hell no," I said, and he squeezed my neck tighter until I gasped. He released his grip and wrapped his fingers around my waist.

"I could smell your scent of arousal filling this room," he breathed, closing his eyes and taking a deep breath. "Omegas are meant to serve their alphas, are they not? To sexually satisfy, to breed, and to fuck."

"No, I don't believe that," I said, my chest rapidly going up and down from my panic. Then, when he released my waist, I ran around him towards the window. I flung the curtain open, letting the sunlight in, and screamed as loud as possible.

No one was coming to my aid. I screamed again and noticed that the Shadow Wolf hadn't even flinched.

"Keep screaming all you want," he said, approaching me again. "I blocked all sound leaving this house. Only the old woman can hear you, but she's not going to do anything about it if she knows what's good for her."

His robe swished audibly around him as he rushed towards me and grasped me by the elbow. In one move, he threw me on the dirty mattress, standing above me as I lay on my back.

"Please," I gasped out. "Just let me go. I promise I'll find you a replacement omega."

"So cute," he chuckled, tracing my thigh with his black boot. "I kind of like you, little omega. You will be mine. To be rutted, bred and mated."

"No, please," I said.

"But first, I need to bring you to your heat," he said. "Since you're not in heat, I will induce your heat using ancient methods."

I sat up, quickly rolling myself into a ball away from this demon. He was crazy and delusional, but he was intent on my destruction. I was sweating profusely, and my chest was going to explode from my rapid breathing.

"Zaneesha, if you can hear me- open the door!" I screamed in one last-ditch effort.

"She's gone now," he said. "Now, remove your clothes."

"No," I said.

"I command you, omega. Remove everything," he ordered. His voice awoke an innate need inside me to obey. To listen instantly or crumple in pain of disappointing my alpha. My hands lifted of their own accord, removing my sweater first as I sat on the filthy mattress. It was like I lost my ability to think as I undressed before him until I sat naked under his watchful eye. "Lay down, omega."

I couldn't do otherwise even if I tried. His alpha compulsion was too powerful for me to fight. Tears streamed down my face as I lay on my back.

Argon knelt in front of me, running his hand down my closed thighs. He traced his finger between the small opening leading to my pulsing core.

"I don't want you," I whispered, terrified whenever his eyes met mine.

"I'm your new master now," he said. "Get used to this. Every night, you will please me, especially during your heat. I will take what's mine and what was promised to me."

I looked around frantically for anything. Any weapon. Anything to help me.

But there was nothing at all.

"You're not my master!" I screamed in frustration.

And that was a big mistake because that set him off.

"Spread your legs. Now," he said, losing patience with me.

My legs slowly spread as if an invisible force was separating them for me. I shouted in frustration, but there was nothing I could do. My omega body was betraying me in every move, wanting to be taken by this powerful alpha. To create the most powerful alphas in the world.

*Omegas were made to procreate.*

He shuffled to move between my legs, his eyes on my pussy. He grasped my thighs, separating them even further as he gazed excitedly at me. I caught sight of his forked tongue flicking, and I recoiled in terror. He wasn't full alpha, but I still obeyed his command. He was something I'd never come across before.

I closed my eyes and felt his tongue flick across my pussy. I shuddered as my pussy came to life under the stroke of his tongue. Each slide and stroke of his tongue caused me to tremble against my better judgment as I gripped the mattress.

"I'll do anything if you let me go," I gasped.

"Then cum for me."

"Not that," I cried out, feeling a wave of pleasure and my stomach clenched. The strokes of his forked tongue were pleasurable as it hit my clit while the other half was inserted into my vagina. I tried to clench my thighs, but his grip held them far apart, opening me as wide as possible for him to lick me and suck me to pleasure.

"Cum for me slutty omega," he growled. His growl sent vibrational waves down my pussy, causing me to scream as I orgasm around his tongue. "Very nice. I knew you could do it. Now onto round two. And this time, you're not allowed to cum."

Panting on the mattress, I opened my eyes and saw him smiling down at me. Fuck, that was creepy. I quickly shut my eyes again. It wasn't so bad with my eyes closed. At least I could feel more pleasure this way. I couldn't imagine the horrors of him mating me and marking me forever as his.

Maybe by then, Caleb would know what his crazy mother had done to me.

Before I could recover, he plunged a finger inside my pussy. I focused on my breathing as he curved his finger, rubbing against the rough patch of skin inside. He plunged his finger in and out of me until I couldn't control my breathing anymore. I was panting at the fifth stroke, wanting to orgasm. When I was almost at the edge of it, he quickly removed his finger and chuckled.

I didn't make a sound. I wanted to groan in frustration. To make him keep going, but I didn't want to give him that pleasure.

"Good, you stopped," I said instead.

"Liar," he said in a silky soft voice. "You want me to keep going. To give you the powerful orgasm you want. That all omegas want from a knot."

I softly whined at the thought of a nice thick knot inside me, and he chuckled.

"I don't want it," I said.

"Stop lying slut," he said again. "Your pussy is leaking all over the mattress, dying for a knot. Don't worry, it'll come. My curved, pierced cock will be deep inside you. We'll wait for your pussy to stop trembling, then we'll go again. By tomorrow you will be in full heat, and you will feel the wrath of my knot."

Terror filled me at the thought. Once I was in heat, I would crave to be knotted by him, and I would be bonded to the devil forever. Birthing hybrid babies for him.

"What the hell are you?"

"A wolf from hell," he muttered as he watched my pussy. "People see me as a devil or the most powerful ancient alpha they'd ever seen.

We will do this again, but with my tongue deep inside you and my fingers pinching your swollen bud. Are you ready for me, my slutty omega?"

# Chapter 27

### Caleb

"I wonder what Jade is thinking now," said Bruce, washing the dishes.

"It's been a day now, and she didn't call or anything," I said, pouring myself a cup of coffee. "I'm prepared to buy a bunch of flowers and return to her parent's house. Is that a good idea?"

"Dude, aren't you going to give up?" asked Nick while flipping through the channels on the TV. "It was embarrassing enough going there the first time. You broke her heart, and now you need to live with it."

"I'm glad he's going again," said Dravin, stretching as he made his way to the living room. "I miss Jade."

"We all do," said Bruce.

"I'm not giving up," I said.

There was no way I was going to give her up that easily. We had a misunderstanding, and that was all. I vowed to win her heart again, whatever it took until she was sick of me. I waited all morning for a call or text. I would provide her with the best life there was, and her fathers would have no need to worry about their daughter.

Suddenly there was frantic knocking at the door.

"Who the hell is that?" said Nick, pulling the door open aggressively. "Caleb, it's your mom."

*What?*

She had never stepped foot in my house before. It must be something important. Abandoning my coffee in the kitchen, I strode towards the door in long strides. My mother rushed inside with tears streaming down her face, more haggard than ever before.

Was it another breakdown?

"Ma, what's wrong?" I asked, trying to stabilize her wobbly body with a hand on her elbow.

"I did something...very bad," she said tearfully, sniffling loudly through her nose.

"What did you do? Come sit down," I guided her over to the sofa, and she perched on the edge of it, refusing to relax. It was probably another one of her delusions.

"The demon was torturing my mind, following me," she started, not making sense as usual. "I had to give him an omega so he could leave me alone."

Alarm bells rang in my head. *Did she do some ritualistic sacrifice or something?*

"What exactly did you do, Ma?" I asked, sounding as calm as possible.

"I gave him your omega, and now I'm wracked with guilt," she said, her words tumbling over each other in her rush.

"What does she mean by that?" Dravin growled, coming to stand next to my mom.

"She's trapped in the guesthouse with the *Shadow Wolf*," she said. "There's no way she can ever leave."

"What the fuck?" said Nick.

"Bruce, keep an eye on my mom," I shouted. "Dravin and Nick, come with me."

"Son, there's no way out for her. He's powerful, and if you take her away from him, he will take revenge," my mom shouted as I ran to the door.

My pulse raced in fear at what my mom could have done.

I needed to get to Jade. She wasn't the Shadow Wolf's. She didn't belong to any other alpha but me. The rain pelted at my face as I ran outside, soaking my hair.

"Jade!" shouted Dravin, knocking on the door furiously.

No sound. Nothing came from the house.

# *Chapter 28*

### Jade

The next morning, I was lying in a pool of my own sweat on the mattress.

My heat had come during the early morning hours after a night of constant near orgasms. Argon hummed a dark song as he stood in front of the window watching the birds feed. He was the oddest fucking male I'd ever met. At times he'd zone out, randomly and it creeped me out each time.

All night, he'd either finger me, suck, or lick my pussy until I was about to climax. Then he stopped every time I screamed in frustration. It would get worse and worse to the point that my heat had taken over my body. And when it did, his smile was the worst I'd ever seen. A look of absolute feral and domination came over his eyes. He liked controlling my body that wished to obey his every command. Every stroke of his tongue or finger took my body to new heights.

Every hour he would do it, giving me a ten-minute break in be-tween. He was brutal and relentless. I was tired and fearful at this point- shaking uncontrollably on the bed.

I was scared when he would knot me. He was biding his time.

My stomach clenched painfully and repeatedly from my heat as it traveled down my pussy. My thighs were covered in a sheen of slick, leaking from me. I was exhausted, in pain, and horny for a knot. But I didn't want his knot. When he found out I was in heat, he roared in victory, and I had never seen his eyes redder.

"You're in heat," he said calmly, turning to me. "Tonight marks the night that I will rut you and mark you as my mate for life. We will wait for the full moon. Isn't that exciting?"

"Why are we waiting for the full moon?"

"It'll give me more powers, and I will use the gravitational pull from the moon to free myself from here," he said, convinced that it would work. I grew terrified at the thought of him escaping this house to wreak havoc on the world with me as his mate. "Do you hear that?"

I strained to hear what he was talking about as I lay there. I could hear faint shouting coming from outside the guesthouse. He was shouting my name over and over. I heard the front door crashing down.

"Caleb," I whispered. He had come for me. My heart soared in my throat, and I wanted to cry. I stood up naked on wobbly legs. "I'm in here!"

"He won't be able to come in," laughed Argon, facing the door. "Soon, you'll scream *my* name when I'm deep inside you."

"Caleb!" I screamed again. I heard pounding on the door.

"Open the door," Caleb roared from outside the door. I heard them kicking the door and wiggling the doorknob. An unearthly orange glow surrounded the door frame, preventing them from entering.

Argon's eyes were glued to the door, fully concentrated on keeping them out.

I ran around the room, looking frantically for a weapon while he wasn't focused on me.

Something. Anything to use as a weapon.

I couldn't find anything except for a metal paperclip on a desk. Snatching it, I ran towards the pentagram drawn on the ground. I looked at Argon and back at the drawing. Then, with clammy hands, I used the paperclip to drag across one of the pentagram lines, breaking the connection.

"What are you doing?!" screamed Argon, turning to me. With his concentration erased, the door finally crashed down. Caleb rushed in, throwing Argon against the wall. Dravin and Nick pounded inside the room. All three of them were holding Argon down.

But Argon was too powerful. He flung them off him one by one, trying to get to me. But Caleb wouldn't let him.

He launched himself at Argon again.

I scratched the pentagram like crazy with the paperclip. My fingers were sore, and my body was in relentless pain from the heat as I was hunched over the image. My nails scraped against the concrete floor as I rubbed off most of the lines from the drawing.

I heard a loud yell, and I looked up.

Argon was vanishing into a cloud of black smoke, black specks and particles hanging in the air as he disappeared back to where he came from.

"Oh my god," I said in relief, collapsing on the ground, still fully naked, but I didn't care.

"Are you okay?" roared Caleb, rushing over to me and kneeling beside me so quickly that I fell onto his arm as he cradled me on the ground. "Jade, talk to me."

"I'll be okay," I said, my throat sore from screaming yesterday and today. No water or food. I was hungry and trembling still from the torture Argon put me through.

"I'm sorry for everything," said Caleb, his voice thick with emotion. "My mom will be punished accordingly. We will take you inside now and give you whatever you need."

"But...," I started to say, but a female's scream interrupted my words. "Oh my god, it's your mom." I jumped off of Caleb's lap, grabbed a sheet from the mattress, and threw it around my body. *Did I do something to hurt her?*

"Stay here with me, Jade," said Nick, grasping my wrist and stopping me from joining Caleb and Dravin rushing out of the door. I tried pulling away from him, but he tightened his grip, pulling me to his chest.

"Let me go," I shouted, pulling away from him. "I've gone through torture and worse. Let me go to her."

Pity filled his eyes as he gazed at me. I was disheveled and worn from last night.

"Okay," he said, holding my hand as we quickly made our way outside.

Even though it was raining outside, the sun on my face was bright, nearly blinding me. I had been indoors for far too long, stuck with the devil himself. Caleb's mother was writhing on the ground, holding her forehead, and screaming outside the guesthouse. Caleb was muttering soothing words, trying to get her to calm down.

"She's having a breakdown again," he explained.

I ran over to her and dropped to my knees next to her.

"It's him. It's Argon torturing her again," I said. I placed my hand on her forehead, and it felt like I was struck by lightning.

Darkness shrouded my vision, and my breathing escalated.

Closing my eyes, I absorbed everything she was feeling. Images of dead omega skeletons in a cave pierced through my mind's eye. Omegas screamed for their lives as he clawed them to death. An image of Caleb on the ground, holding his dead wife in his hands, and a cackle sounded deep in my mind.

Argon was enjoying this.

Flooding my mind with images of the tortured and dead omegas.

"Jade, Jade!" I could hear the alphas shouting. They sounded far away, muffled like an underwater chorus.

My hand on her forehead felt like it was glued to her as pressure surrounded us, keeping us under his control.

"Leave her," I commanded the presence, trying to snap back into reality. Instead, the images in my brain whirled faster and faster until I could barely breathe. "Leave us alone! Leave her. You're not welcome here!"

My heart was racing, and my palms clammy as I fought for my life and her life.

"She has a debt to pay," Argon snickered. I shook my head wildly, and Caleb's mother screamed with some invisible pain he inflicted.

"She doesn't owe you anything."

"I made a promise to him that if he helped us, I owed him," said Zaneesha.

*What?*

"Get out of her mind," I shouted, pressing my hand tighter on her forehead, projecting strength into her. "Think of your happiest moment. Don't pay attention to what he's throwing at you. Please Zaneesha. Come back."

"I can't," she groaned. I opened my eyes and stared deep into her struggling face. Her pupils were dilated, and she looked ready to collapse.

"Don't listen to him," I shouted. "He's nothing. He's weak and powerless."

"No, he's right. I deserve it," she said, trembling all over. "I had a premonition that he would be evil, yet I brought him back to life."

"And he *is* evil," I said, even though I felt sick.

"I should let him take me," she said, shuddering.

"This is what you deserve," whispered the male voice into our minds.

"Don't let it control you," I shouted over his voice.

Tears rolled down her face as she scrunched her eyebrows in pain.

I heard an invisible male shriek in the air as Zaneesha's eyes opened wider, focused on me. Concentrating with all her strength.

"Leave me alone," she whispered, with barely any force in her words. When his hold began to diminish, her next command was stronger. "Leave Argon!"

Suddenly, I felt the invisible force burst around us. The heavy feeling over my body disappeared, and a calm, tranquil feeling fell over me. I took deep calming breaths, slowly removing my hand from her forehead. Zaneesha sat up from the ground, also regaining her breath.

"It's gone. Do you feel that?" I asked her, smiling as I laid a hand on her forearm.

"It is," she said, her voice trembling. Tears flowed down her face as she hugged my sheet-covered body. "I'm sorry. I'm so sorry."

"It's okay. I understand why you did it," I said. "He's way too powerful."

"Thank you," she gasped out, touching my face. "I don't know how Caleb found someone like you. Your inner strength and soft heart saved us both. You didn't need to save me, and I am indebted to you."

She turned to Caleb who was sitting quietly watching us, and hugged him next. I pulled the sheets tighter around me, hunched in pain.

"Are you okay?" asked Bruce, who I didn't notice was beside me the entire time.

"I'm in heat," I gasped out.

"Carry her inside. Now," said Caleb, panic written all over his face.

# Chapter 29

### Jade

I was in Dravin's arms, delirious with pain as he bounded up the stairs.

We were in Caleb's room, and he gently placed me on the bed. Dravin, Nick, and Bruce surrounded me as Caleb attended to his mother outside. I groaned as a wave of pain squeezed down my belly and my core.

"Let us give you some relief Jade," said Dravin.

"No," I said harshly, curling up pain as another wave of pain struck my body.

"Caleb isn't here," said Bruce, knowing that I felt reluctant about their pack leader. The thought of relief from these relentless attacks that Argon brought on was appealing.

"I can't," I cried out when my stomach clenched again at the emptiness within me. "I'll ride out the heat, and if I'm about to die, I'll let you know."

"Jade, don't do this," Dravin said, sitting beside me. His voice was thick and full of pain. He laid a comforting hand on my back. "Don't hurt yourself over your differences with Caleb. We care for you deeply. This is hurting us as much as it's hurting you."

"Please give me time to think about this," I gasped. "I'll call for you if I need you. Argon didn't listen to me, so will you?"

"Fuck that hurts," said Dravin. "We'll leave you alone for a little bit and give you space to think. I'll be right downstairs."

I nodded slightly.

When they all left the room, guilt hit me. I shouldn't be feeling guilty. But they sounded sincere, unlike Argon.

I needed a shower badly. I smelled like smoke and ash. Argon's touch and caress had to be erased. With immense strength, I got up from the bed, the dirty sheet dropping to the ground. I didn't have my towel or anything. I desperately needed to get under the water. I limped to the bathroom while holding my middle. I was slow, but I made it inside, shutting the door behind me. With one hand gripping the counter, I twisted the golden faucet until the shower came on.

Standing under the running cold water relieved my stress but not the pain. The pain worsened in my belly as I scrubbed my hair with Nick's coconut-scented shampoo. I tried to rinse my hair quickly but doubled over in pain, letting out a small yelp.

God, my first heat was too much. I hated this.

"Are you okay in there?" said Caleb, bursting into the bathroom, seeing me sitting under the spray of water, curled up in pain. "It's your heat, isn't it?"

He came over to me, pushing my wet hair back from my face, calmly squeezing and rinsing the remainder of the shampoo from my hair. He rubbed soap down my back, carefully washing it in circles.

"What are you doing?"

"I'll finish washing you. Just relax," he said close to my ear.

I was self-conscious of my naked state, but it wasn't like he'd never seen me naked. I held my middle, sitting in the bathtub as he washed and rinsed me.

"Thank you," I said in a low voice, and he kissed me on the forehead. His kiss felt like a warm hug. An oasis of protection and safety. I couldn't let the warm feelings overwhelm me. He helped me stand as he carefully wrapped a clean towel around me, drying me off.

"You're trembling," he said, studying me as I stepped out of the tub. "What did that bastard do to you?"

I shook my head silently. Then unable to contain it anymore, tears rolled down my face as a feeling of helplessness struck me.

Caleb hugged me to his chest.

His scent of the trees filled my senses, giving me life again. The feeling of hope again. He hugged me tight as I cried and shuddered against his chest.

"I'm sorry," I blubbered, but he only hugged me tight.

"You're safe with me, baby," he muttered. I felt the vibrational wave of his purring as he softly comforted me as I cried. When the tears stopped, I pulled away embarrassed, wiping my eyes with the towel.

"It was horrible," I hiccuped as I blew my nose into a tissue that Caleb handed me. I watched Caleb's face turn to fury as I described the night. The devil's intensity to bring me to heat. The near-climaxing on repeat for hours on end until my heat came.

"I'm so so sorry, sweetheart," he said, all sincerity in his voice. "I will never let something like that happen to you ever again."

I wrapped my towel around me tighter in the foggy bathroom. Caleb's touches had soothed my pain a tiny bit, but it was coming back in full force. Taking a deep breath, I approached Caleb and rested a hand on his chest, covered with a gray shirt.

"Will you help me through my heat?" I asked. I wasn't sure if I was making the right move at all. I just knew I couldn't live with this pain for the next few hours. It was unbearable, and it hurt like hell.

"Do you trust me?" he asked, placing his hand over mine. I felt his heart beating under my palm. "I am nothing like the monster that you were trapped with. Do you trust that I will never hurt you? Because after I rut you, I want you to be my mated omega. Forever."

My pulse raced as I stared into his eyes. He was being serious about me for once. He wasn't playing games, and I could sense it.

"I trust you," I whispered. He was saying everything that I'd dreamt of over my lonely nights.

"I never meant to match you with another pack after that night," he explained. "You might not believe me, but I promise you that I was fully intending to cancel with them and keep you for myself."

I swallowed, remembering how seeing those texts pained me.

"Okay," I said, my heart softening towards him again. My wishful omega heart was so weak against this pack that it was ridiculous. "Am I being stupid?"

"No, you're not," he said, kissing me soundly on the lips with my hand over his heart. I felt his heart beating faster as his lips pressed over mine. "Do you feel my heart?"

"I do."

"Then you know the truth of how you make me feel."

## Caleb

Jade was a vision to behold as I gazed upon her naked body on the bed.

Dravin held her right leg open while Nick held onto her left leg. Her weeping pussy displayed in the middle for me made my cock harden like never before. I stood naked before her, gazing at her face while Bruce rained kisses on her neck while palming her breasts. Her long black hair fanned around my pillow, her lips cherry red as she bit her lower lip nervously.

"Please, Caleb," she breathed, her face pink and flushed. Her small hand was on her belly. I could see she was in pain even though she tried to hide it from us. My cock was hard and ready. Ready to penetrate her tight little hole as it quivered under my gaze.

"Yes," I said, immediately climbing onto the bed to join them.

Nick and Dravin rubbed her inner thighs when I approached her. My dick stood straight out, ready to impregnate this omega.

She was mine. Or I would make her mine after this.

She would know who her alpha was after I knotted her. As I knelt between her legs, I took a good look at her pussy. Spreading her pussy lips open, I saw how bright pink it was. Her body heat was high, and I could see her little hole opening and closing, waiting for me.

Gripping my hard cock in my hand, I lined it up to her pussy, touching her with it. She groaned as I teased her entrance.

"No games, please," she moaned, eagerly lifting her hips.

No, I wasn't like that asshole Argon. I would give her the release and the pleasure she deserved.

I pushed into her, and her breasts bounced at the impact. *Damn*, my dick felt so good inside her tight heated hole. I was going to be her first during her heat, and I was honored.

"Do you like this, little omega?" I asked as I pushed deeper inside of her.

"Yes, it feels so good, Caleb," she said, gazing at me with wonder and admiration in her eyes. I plunged deeper into her and thrust into her tight channel as it hugged my cock. I was already about to orgasm since it had been a while, but I held on. She needed a good fucking after being teased to death in that hellhole.

Nick reached down, his fingers strumming her clit as I pounded into her heated slit.

"Does this feel good?" asked Nick.

I groaned as her pussy squeezed tight around my cock waiting impatiently for my knot.

"It feels so good. Keep doing it like that, Nick," she breathed. "In circles with your thumb. Oh, moons."

When her pussy squeezed my cock tight again, I dropped my head to her shoulder, softly nicking her skin with my sharp incisors.

"Oh," she gasped when I marked her at last.

"My *mate*," I whispered. "My omega. Say it, baby."

"I'm yours," she breathed, wincing from the bite as her pussy clenched tightly around my cock. I allowed myself to finally explode inside of her. My liquid spurted deep inside her belly. Just as I liked. My usually controlled breathing was erratic as I huffed and puffed over her curvy body.

I licked the tiny droplet of blood from her shoulder.

"Be ready for my knot," I said, kissing her on the lips. My cock slowly swelled inside of her from the base, filling her up to bring her relief. "How do you feel, baby?"

"So much better," she said, smiling for the first time since we pulled her out of the guesthouse. "I didn't think a knot would bring me instant relief like this."

"See?" I said, kissing the smile on her luscious pink lips. "We're here to serve you. To protect you and to fulfill your every need. Every alpha around you right now is ready to knot you and help you through your heat."

"I understand now," she said softly, giggling when Bruce bit her earlobe. "Bruce, stop."

"Sorry, honey," Bruce said. "After Caleb's knot goes down, I'll take you next."

"We can take her at the same time," said Dravin.

"I guess I can play with her pussy until it's my turn," sighed Nick. He was always the last one since he was quiet.

"Nick, it's always better to have it one-on-one," I winked as I sunk my knot deeper into Jade's pussy. Nice and tight with just my cock in her.

Nick smiled widely.

"I know."

# Chapter 30

### Jade

I nestled underneath Caleb while his knot held me in place.

Bruce on one side and Dravin on the other side kissing my arms and thighs while praising every inch of me felt wonderful. I basked in their admiration of me as they explored my body while Caleb kissed my breasts.

"So pretty," said Caleb, enjoying the way my breasts bounced when he sucked and let go. Desire swept through me again, tightening in my belly as his knot began releasing me. "You're mated to us now. Officially our omega."

His mark would ensure that no other alpha pack would come near or claim me.

"Hell yeah," said Bruce.

"I never thought I'd ever move on after the death of my last mate," said Caleb, opening up to me. I touched his chest gently. Showing him that it was safe to talk about it. "My heart feels at peace now. The past will stay in the past."

"I agree," I said.

"I love you," he said, kissing me on the lips again. My heart swelled with hope and more love for him.

He actually said the words. *Should I tell him how I felt?* I was his omega now, so it didn't matter.

"I love you too," I said.

"How about me?" asked Dravin, who was grabbing my arm threateningly.

"You too," I giggled. "All of you."

"When did you know?" asked Bruce, running his thumb down my hips.

"Ever since I went back," I said. "I couldn't stop thinking about all of you."

"We couldn't stop thinking about you, too," said Caleb. "The pack was driving me nuts about you."

My heart was beating fast after my confession, but I felt good finally saying it. The bed was warm and toasty as the pack touched my body. Nick was softly licking my toes, and I gasped in surprise.

"Your little feet are so pretty," he said, rubbing his thumb over the colorful red polish on my big toe. "So cute."

"Thank you," I blushed. I wasn't used to this attention, and I wondered if I would be used to it at all. Hands, fingers, and lips all over my body felt so wrong but so good at the same time. Exactly what an omega like myself needed.

"God," grunted Dravin as he pumped his cock with one hand while rubbing my thigh with his other hand. "You almost done there, Caleb?"

"Yes," said Caleb, kissing me one last time before rolling off me.

The temporary relief from Caleb's knot was short-lived. After a couple of minutes, I groaned in pain again as Nick pressed on my belly.

"I know it hurts," said Nick, purring into my ear. His long hair brushed my face as he snuggled near me, bringing me comfort in the warm bed. "Dravin and Bruce will take care of you now. Then I'll take you last. Does two big knots- one inside your ass and one in your pussy sound delicious?"

"Yes. Yes, it does," I gasped when my pussy squeezed around nothing. "Dravin, hurry. I need you inside me."

He lifted my legs over his shoulders in a business-like manner. Ready to take action.

"Is your pussy ready for me?" Dravin muttered as he gazed long and hard at the wetness between my legs. He swirled the cum from Caleb around my pussy, mixing it in with my slick. My face heated.

"I can get cleaned up first," I offered, trying to close my legs. But he pinned my legs open so I couldn't close them.

"I want you just like this. You're perfect," Dravin rasped. "Your pussy dripping with his semen makes me hard as fuck."

I was shocked by his words.

"You're blushing," said Bruce, rubbing my ass.

Dravin's dirty talk turned me on even more than I was already.

"Oh my," I whimpered when Dravin's cock speared into me. He was pretty sizeable, stretching me wide around him. Bruce pinched my ass, and I yelped. When I jumped, it forced Dravin's cock to go inside me even deeper.

"I want your ass," Bruce grunted in my ear, full of lust and desire for me. I shivered with anticipation.

"We'll take her between us," said Dravin, lifting me off the bed, and I wrapped my arms around him. My legs tightened around his waist for balance. His hands cupped my ass. When Bruce came around behind me, Dravin spread my cheeks for him.

"Beautiful," said Bruce as his thumb ran across my crack, brushing past my anus. I trembled in Dravin's arms, his cock pinned into my pussy, holding me up between the two of them. Bruce's thumb settled over my anus, gently rubbing over it in circles. Warmth began pooling in my bottom the more he rubbed. Fuck, I was going to slick from my butt again. It was shameful to me for some reason, and I clenched my butt. "Slick for me, baby."

"I can't," I lied, trying to focus on the thick rod nestled in my pussy. Dravin began to lift me by the hips, up and down, spearing me with his cock. Bruce rubbed my butt cheeks in circles with both hands, each time stopping at my crack to stroke my anus.

"Slick for me, Jade," Bruce commanded with more urgency. His thumb pressed around my hole, all around the sphincter. He wasn't letting up. A sudden shot of heat streamed through me, erupting from my ass, and I cried out from the sole delight of it. He rubbed the slick around my ass, pressing his thumb inside my opening, stretching me open for his cock. I couldn't even handle him in my pussy, the night I rode him. He sensed my worry, kissing my neck. "Don't be scared, baby. You were made for this."

"Yes," groaned Dravin, his gaze burning into my soul. He lifted me higher each time he brought me over his thick rod. "Such a sexy omega."

My heart tripled in size, and my pussy clenched tight around him.

Before I knew it, Bruce had pushed himself into my asshole as it stretched naturally for him. I felt so full in both holes as both alphas penetrated deeper into me. My ass was being stretched to the limit, and my pussy was hugging Dravin's cock like it would be the last time I would get a dick inside me.

"Your hole is nice and snug," said Bruce as he slowly speared into my butt. Slick dripped from my pussy and my ass in my frenzy to orgasm. All this stimulation was fucking killing me. I never knew that a cock inside my butt would make me go wild like this. The heat and warmth of their bodies as I was sandwiched in the middle felt so good.

"Pound into my butt," I begged.

And he did.

Bruce pulled his cock back and thrust into me with full force, making my breasts bounce high. Dravin licked his lips at the sight.

"At the same time," said Dravin. "Hold on, Bruce. Let's see how high her breasts can fly."

"No!" I screamed as I felt both of their muscular frames move back, both cocks pulling away. Then in the next second, they both slammed into me, sending me into the air with their hands gripping my waist. My boobs bounced high in the air, and Dravin groaned in satisfaction.

"Fucking hot," he said. My pussy and ass were getting sore from their rough assault. But it felt so good. "Again."

"Ahh," I yelled again when they collided into me again. A cock in my ass and a cock in my pussy, ravaging me like nothing else. On the next stroke, I screamed when I felt my pussy and ass clenching tight. They slammed into me again. The familiar tightness and release as I squirted all over their cocks. My slick spurted from my pussy and my ass. "Oh, my god."

"Oh yes," said Bruce when he felt my anus clenching around his penis. "Beautiful little squirter."

"Fuck yes," groaned Dravin, his cock stilling as he climaxed. His hot juices exploded directly into my belly, his cock knotting immediately to hold all the semen.

"Yes, clench tighter, baby," Bruce said, as I held onto Dravin tightly even though I felt like collapsing. I felt drained after my powerful orgasm, but I clenched around Bruce's raging cock. "Clench for me again."

I clenched my ass with all my strength around his relentless cock.

"Good girl," he grunted as he exploded into my anus. "I'm going to knot inside your little butt."

"That feels so good," I moaned as I felt both of them knotting both holes. I felt so satisfied like never before. They carried me over to the bed, sandwiching me between them as we lay on our sides. Dravin faced me in the front while Bruce spooned me from behind, his cock swelling even more inside my ass. Nick began rubbing my feet as soon as I was on the bed.

Caleb whistled. He had been watching the entire time I was getting screwed by two of his alphas.

"Good job," he said, getting up from the bed. "She'll be satisfied for a little while."

"Oh goodness," I said sleepily as I yawned, resting my head against Dravin's hairy chest. "You have red chest hair."

"That's because my hair is red, my sleepy omega," chuckled Dravin.

Bruce rubbed my back in lazy circles as he kissed my shoulders. "You did such a good job, Jade."

"Thank you," I mumbled, my eyes slowly closing. The relief from the heat of pain would be short, but I wanted to take a quick nap. After all, I couldn't sleep last night with the devil in the room with me. "I'm sleepy."

Caleb gave me water with a straw while I lay there with my eyes closed. The cool water felt amazing on my parched throat.

"It's okay. Get some rest, babe," said Dravin, his fingers stroking my hair as he purred into me.

The vibrations from his purrs and Bruce's petting were enough to send me off to a deep sleep.

Upon waking up, the pain was shooting down my belly to my privates.

*Fuck.* My heat wasn't over with yet.

My eyes snapping open, I saw that the room was empty except for Nick lying on his back next to me, stroking his hard penis. He was completely naked and ready to fuck when needed. It was dark outside, and I realized I had gone for hours without a knot inside me.

"Are you up for service?" I croaked, half-joking and half-serious. But mostly serious.

"You're awake," he said, turning to me. His honey-blond hair brushed against my nude body as he climbed on top of me. "Of course, I'm up for service. I aim to please."

I wanted to laugh, but I couldn't. I was clutching my belly in pain as it spasmed from the emptiness inside me.

"I need your knot, please."

"Turn on your back. Here I'll help you," his hands gripped my waist, flipping me over onto my back. "Open up for me."

"I can't," I moaned. It hurt even more to stretch. Omegas weren't joking about these heats. I vowed never to forget another heat suppressant in the future.

"I'll help you. Tell me if it hurts," he said.

"It hurts all over," I groaned as he gripped my thighs.

"Where is fucking Caleb when you need him for once," he muttered, probably wondering how to deal with a crazed sex-starved omega like myself.

"I'm sorry," I said, gasping. My chest rose and fell dramatically as I allowed him to separate my legs apart.

"It's okay, baby," said Nick. "Should we do some foreplay?"

"No! Please just stick it in," I said as my belly contracted harder this time. I needed him to knot inside me as soon as possible. Sweat beaded down my back as I opened my legs wider for him, my slick dripping down onto the bed in my frustration. His face was turning pink from the pressure. I turned around onto my belly, presenting my bottom to him. "Rut me like this."

"Okay, babe," he said, gripping my bottom. I knew he was the youngest of the pack and was probably intimidated by me being much older. But I needed him to take charge, and me not facing him could help. "Doggy-style it is."

I felt him spread my ass cheeks apart, and suddenly his penis jammed deep into my pussy. I groaned in pleasure as I felt him bury his cock in deeper.

"Fuck me, Nick. Don't be gentle with me."

"I'll fuck you until you can barely walk," he promised.

He pulled out and then back in with such force that the sound of his sack slapping against my ass echoed in the room.

"*Moons*, yes," I moaned.

"Your little pussy is trembling around my cock," he growled in my ear, his body on top of mine. The heat of skin pressing against my heated skin. Every touch and thrust sent me higher. He pistoned into me again, his hairy thighs rubbing against mine with each thrust. "Is my cock feeding your pussy, good?"

"Yes."

"Say yes, alpha," he said in a low voice, nicking my shoulder with his teeth. The pain felt good. He brought his hand around my legs, finding my clit that he had been touching all day. "That's what I am to you."

"Yes, alpha."

I let out another moan as he rubbed my clit with every stroke of his thick cock inside of me. Around and around, his finger covered every crevice of my pussy as it squelched loudly from my slick.

"Sorry," I said, embarrassed.

"Don't ever apologize about that," he growled, pressing his finger even harder on my pussy. He took my hand, leading it to my clit. "Keep rubbing yourself, baby. I'm going to slam into you now."

His cock pushed deeper inside of me as I fingered myself. I tried to do what he did, and I swirled my fingers around my clit. My fingers touched his massive bulge nestled into my pussy. My pussy clenched happily around his thick appendage. I rubbed my clit faster and harder, slowly taking myself to new heights despite the pain in my belly. I saw fireworks as I clenched tight around him in one powerful orgasm.

"Good job, honey," he said. One more powerful thrust, and he let out a jet of hot liquid deep inside me, climaxing at the same time. His cock was finally knotting inside of me, and I sighed in relief, collapsing onto the bed. Nick's body weight on my back sent tingles of warmth within me. "Better?"

"Yes," I said. "Sorry that was intense."

"It's okay. Don't ever be sorry."

"Where's everyone else?"

I didn't think to ask him while I was in mortal pain, but now that I had calmed down a bit, I was able to think clearly.

"They're getting the new house ready," he answered. "We're supposed to move in tonight so we can have a bigger space for you."

"Oh," I said, feeling a little bit sad. I'd prefer all of them here with me in this tiny room, which I didn't mind.

"They'll be back soon," he said, squeezing my butt. "Don't be sad."

"I'm not," I protested.

"I can smell your scent, baby," he said, kissing me on the cheek. "I know when your emotions change."

"Well...I just want them with me. I should shut up. I'm getting greedy."

"No, you've never been in heat, right? This isn't something you're used to," he said.

"Were you guys used to this from your past relationship?" I asked, curious.

"Not at all," he said. "We never got the chance to get her through a heat. That's why we don't have any babies."

"Oh god," I said, realizing I could get pregnant right now while his knot pumped his semen inside me. "What if I get pregnant? The heat suppressants I took last week might not work."

"And so? You have us now," he purred, calming me down. "I can't wait to see your belly nice and round with the baby I put inside you. Should we discuss baby names?"

"No," I groaned, and he chuckled.

# Chapter 31

### Jade

"Ready?" Nick asked.

I was wrapped in a comfortable bathrobe after he had helped me take a bath before driving me to the new home in his car. I was sitting in the passenger side, and he went around the car, opening the door for me. I tried to get up but doubled over when my stomach muscles clenched again.

"I hate this," I groaned, gripping the door tight.

"I'll carry you inside," said Nick, the gentleman that he was.

"I've got her," I heard Caleb saying as he came up behind Nick.

"They're all here," I said happily.

"Yeah," said Nick, sounding unhappy as Caleb leaned into the car, wrapping his hands around me.

Caleb's scent washed over me as he lifted me in his arms, cradling me tight. My stomach growled, and as I watched his jaw tense.

"I have food prepared," he grunted, walking in quick strides across the driveway and towards the home.

"But I'm in too much pain," I said. "I can't eat right now. I need a knot."

He shook his head adamantly.

"Fine, I will have Bruce knot inside you next while I feed you."

That thought made me blush so hard I could swear he could feel the heat radiate off my face.

"Okay," I said in a little voice.

He strode into the house, and I heard hammering on the wall upstairs. I looked around the living room and noticed all my designs stayed the same.

"We didn't change much," he said as if reading my mind. "We prepared the master bedroom for you, though. It's a surprise."

I didn't decorate any of the rooms upstairs and wondered what they did to them.

"Ooh," I said excitedly.

We approached the very last room down the hall, and he twisted the doorknob open. My mouth flew open when the first thing I saw were my paintings hung all over the walls. I couldn't speak. My hand flew to my mouth in stunned silence.

There was a huge bed in the middle covered in white sheets, sitting underneath my best painting of an omega staring out at the ocean with the mark of a wolf claw on her shoulder. I couldn't believe they'd done all this for me. The silver curtains matched the intricate silver design on the giant headboard. And the best part were the silver cushions in the corner surrounded by canvas paper and painting supplies.

My nest. *This was my home now.*

My heart couldn't take it anymore as tears rolled from my eyes and goosebumps formed on my skin.

"Do you like it?" asked Bruce, who was standing on a ladder with a hammer in one hand. The entire pack had gone silent, watching my reaction.

"I love it," I whispered. "I can't even talk because of how touched I am. I can't believe you all did this for me."

"You're worth the effort, my darling," said Bruce.

Caleb sat on the large cozy silver chair with me on his lap like I was a baby. It felt weird, but it also felt natural to me that he would do that.

"I'm glad you like the room," said Caleb, dabbing at my tears with a napkin. "Nick, could you prepare a plate of food for our beautiful omega? Bruce, you will knot her while I feed her."

The pain had come back in full force, temporarily forgotten by the shock of the beautiful room covered in my paintings.

"I can knot her instead," volunteered Dravin, standing at the bottom of the ladder handing Bruce supplies.

Bruce hit him on the head with his free hand.

"She needs a *big* knot," he said snidely.

"I'm taking her next, though," said Dravin, licking his lips as he gazed at me.

"Don't worry, I can take any knot I can get," I muttered through my pain. "Get in line."

I was curled on Caleb's lap as he got up to deposit me on the bed for Bruce.

"Let me wash my hands quick," said Bruce, his heavy footsteps disappearing down the hall. I desperately wanted to call my family and tell them what was happening, but it was too embarrassing. It was a momentous occasion to go into heat, but at the same time, my parents didn't know that I was screwing four guys all day.

Dravin lay next to me while Nick was downstairs getting food. I wondered how I would eat and get knotted. I've never done it before, so the concept seemed foreign to me. My bathrobe was coming loose, and I tore it off because of how hot my skin was during this heat.

"Damn," said Dravin, drinking in the sight of my naked body lying on the bed next to him. "Your thighs are so shapely. Makes me want to bang you before Bruce gets back. Actually, how about I do just that?"

He lifted me over on top of him before I could protest.

"Dravin, no. He'll get so mad," I giggled as his cock slid inside me while I was on top.

"He can get mad all he wants," growled Dravin, ramming his cock deeper inside me. Staking his claim. My eyes rolled back in my head as I started to move back and forth on him. He gripped my waist, bouncing me on his cock. "Up and down."

"Like this?"

"Just like that baby," he groaned, his face twisted in ecstasy. "You feel so fucking good on my cock."

"Oh, Dravin," I moaned as I felt his cock sinking deeper into me the more I rode him. Easing his heavy rod inside of me never felt so good while I was on top.

"What the hell are you doing?" Bruce demanded as he strode into the room.

"Bruce, it's okay," I said, my voice throaty with arousal. "I want your knot next."

"You'll have it right now," said Bruce.

"What are you doing, big man?" said Dravin, annoyed that I was getting distracted.

"I'll knot inside her ass," said Bruce as I heard his belt slap to the ground. The metal of the belt clinked against the bedpost. My heart pounded hard. I've never seen Bruce so pissed off before. "You're not getting her alone."

"Fuck off," said Dravin as Bruce climbed into the bed behind me.

My pulse raced as he spread my ass cheeks apart, fingering my anus. I felt his finger press inside me, stretching me.

I yelped, but he continued to insert his finger inside my ass. He was rushing it, so Dravin didn't have me for himself. Every time Dravin lifted me up to drop me on his cock, Bruce's finger would slide in and out of my asshole.

"Bruce," I shouted, and he finally popped his finger out from my behind.

"Are you ready for my dick inside your ass?" he said, positioning himself over Dravin's legs to get to me. He stretched my ass open, and my eyes widened. These were all alphas, and if one stepped over the other one, there was hell to pay. Dravin exploded inside of me, his cock stilling as it released his liquid.

When he began to knot inside me, I breathed a sigh of relief.

Bruce was pushing his large cock inside of my tiny asshole, and I groaned as I felt a few inches of him strain to go inside. My slick wasn't enough back there, and I heard him spit on his cock to wedge the rest of it inside my ass.

Caleb and Nick came in with two plates of food at that moment.

"What happened here?" said Caleb, taking in the sight of me sitting on top of Dravin, all knotted up, and Bruce penetrating me from behind with his giant cock. Then, slowly, my ass eased around him, allowing Bruce to thrust in and out of me.

My pussy throbbed as Dravin's knot thickened inside of me, holding me in place while Bruce took my ass. Caleb brought a forkful of lasagna to my mouth.

"Open up," said Caleb. I opened my mouth and savored the delicious red sauce.

"Mhm," I said, while Bruce pumped into my ass. Caleb fed me bite after bite of the delicious lasagna. The knot in my pussy felt so good, relieving my pain while I ate. Bruce roared as he came inside my ass, pulling out his cock before he could knot inside. "I'm so comfortable right now."

"That's good, baby," said Caleb as I adjusted myself over Dravin's knot as Dravin snickered under me- his hands playing with my breasts. Bruce's cock dripped in white liquid as he finished himself off.

"Why didn't you knot inside me Bruce?" I asked with my mouth full. I quickly covered my mouth, wondering what got into me.

"Eat up, baby," said Caleb, feeding me another bite rapidly and not allowing me to take a break between bites. I was starving anyway, so it was welcome.

"I wanted you to keep eating," said Bruce. "If I knotted inside your ass, you would be uncomfortable."

"What a thoughtful alpha," said Dravin sarcastically.

"Fuck you," said Bruce.

"Settle down," said Caleb, feeding me another bite. I leaned against Dravin's chest, exhausted, full, and finally satiated. Caleb felt my forehead with the back of his hand. "You're less hot and past the critical stages."

"Thank goodness," I sighed on Dravin's chest. Nick wiped my mouth with a napkin, and I smiled weakly at him. A burst of love shot through me. "You're so amazing, Nick. You too, Dravin. And you, Bruce."

Caleb lifted his eyebrows jokingly.

"And of course, you too, Cal," I said, snuggling my head under Dravin's neck.

He lifted an arm around me, holding me tight against him as we waited for his knot to recede and set me free. But in the meantime, I wanted it in there nice and snug to keep my pain away.

"You're more amazing than we could ever dream of," said Bruce, kissing me. I felt Caleb's and Nick's kisses rain down my body as I closed my eyes, my lips turning up in a smile.

# Epilogue

### *Nine Months Later*
### Jade

My belly was heavy with pregnancy as I lay in my nest. I was alone in the room, having been lethargic and tired lately to hang out with the rest of my alpha pack downstairs. After my heat, we found out I was pregnant two weeks later, and the joy on my alphas' faces was infectious. It would be their first baby ever. We chose not to find out the gender, but now I was regretting it as I lay there despondently, paintbrush in my hand. We weren't as prepared as we should be.

I was due next week, and I couldn't wait.

The sun shined into the room, doing nothing to brighten my mood and all the aches I felt. My alphas were worried about me, took care of every food craving I had, and made my aches easier to deal with calming purr sessions from each alpha. My favorite was my nightly massages from Nick and bath times with Caleb.

"Jade? Are you awake?" asked Caleb, walking into the room. He looked fresh in his black suit, his long hair back tied back.

"Yes."

"Why aren't you getting ready for our date?" he asked, kneeling outside my cushioned nest. He had a concerned look on his face. Normally I would get excited when we went out as a pack on our many dates.

"I'm just feeling a little more tired than usual," I said, trying to get up, but he grasped my hand right away, helping me up. My belly was heavy, and all my joints ached to death.

"Should we cancel?" he asked, peering into my face and giving me a peck on the lips. His hand rubbed my belly as I leaned against him.

"No way," I said. I knew if I canceled, I would feel sad for the rest of the night, and all the alphas were getting ready. I stood on my tiptoes to give him a real kiss on the lips. "Stop worrying, Caleb. You're always worrying about me, babe."

"Because I love you," he said, his eyes softening. "Our baby looks ready to come out."

"Not for another week," I groaned, placing my hand over his as he rubbed my belly. I felt my stomach tense, and I paused for moment, wincing.

"You okay, babe?"

"It's not the real contraction," I said. "Nothing to worry about."

When the contraction passed, I breathed a sigh of relief. If these were Braxton-Hick's contractions, I couldn't imagine what the real one would feel like.

For our evening date, I wore a sparkling plum-colored gown showing off my pregnant belly. It was a light dress that didn't cling too tight to my body. I looked into the tiny compact mirror while I sat in the back of the van with Nick to my left and Dravin to my right.

"You look beautiful," said Nick, rubbing my forearm.

I rubbed off some of the eye makeup. I didn't know what I was thinking applying so much eyeliner. My hair was done in a high ponytail, making me look regal. This would be our last night out before the baby arrived, so I wanted to look my very best.

"He's right, baby. You look stunning as always," said Dravin, whose eyes were on me the moment I came downstairs to join them.

"Aww, thank you," I said, closing my mirror and stuffing it into the designer purse by Glo-mega Nick bought me. I looked up, seeing that we were driving towards the ocean. "Where are we going? I thought we were going to a restaurant. I would have dressed more casually."

"It's a surprise, honey," called Bruce from the front seat.

"You guys are always surprising me," I said, smiling.

"Our favorite thing to do," said Dravin, his eyes on my lips. "May I kiss those pretty lips of yours?"

I nodded, and he dove right in, pressing his lips against mine. His hand carefully curled around my neck, not messing up my hair. I absorbed his scent and cologne for the night, drugging me as I breathed in deeply. I loved my alpha's scents even more after becoming pregnant. Most smells repelled me, but I craved to be cuddled, held, and kissed by my pack. When I pulled away, I was breathless with desire.

"I need to fix my lipstick now," I said, pulling my purple lipstick out from my purse.

"Damn, sorry, baby."

"It's okay," I said, applying a new coat.

"We're here," said Caleb.

Looking up, I saw what looked like a wharf. As we stepped out, I gasped when I saw a large yacht sitting in the ocean before us. It was docked with the captain in front, looking at us expectantly.

"Oh my god, what did you do, Caleb?" I asked, astonished. I had never been on a yacht before, and it looked too luxurious. The white sails flew in the wind, a stunning sight to behold. It was sleek and modern, with floor-to-ceiling windows.

"We're going to spend the evening on that," said Caleb, holding my left hand while Dravin held onto my right.

"This is so crazy," I said, gazing at the water. "And romantic!"

Bruce chuckled at my words, and Caleb kissed me on the cheek.

"Shall we go?" said Caleb.

We made our way to the deck, with the captain welcoming us on board. I saw many people onboard and gasped when I saw my friends and family there. I looked at Caleb excitedly, and he winked at me. He organized all this for me last minute, and to think he gave me the option to cancel...I couldn't imagine if I had canceled. My mom rushed over to me, hugging me with a twinkle in her eye.

She had been supportive throughout my pregnancy, coming to our place multiple times a week to cook and help out. If not for my mother and Keera, I would have felt alone during my pregnancy.

After I mated with the pack of my dreams, I could swear my relationship with my mom had gotten better. I was no longer living the life she ordained, and finding myself had strengthened my confidence. I was able to open up more, and so did she.

"Hey, Mom," I said, matching her smile. "I can't believe we're on this yacht. What are you doing here?"

"Your alphas invited me and your fathers," she said.

"Wow."

"Your alphas are doing an amazing job," she said. "Come say hi to your fathers."

I hugged each of my dads and caught up with them for the first twenty minutes of the trip. Then I spoke to Keera next. Her alpha Jatix's arm was around her.

"Where is the rest of your pack?" I asked her.

"Shawn gets seasick, and the rest of them are working," said Keera, looking up at Jatix with adoration. He gave her a one-sided smile and kissed her on the lips. I smiled at how cute they were together.

"You look ready to pop," Keera said, her eyes wide when she noticed my belly.

"I feel like I am," I said.

"Why won't you find out what the baby is?" asked Keera, who was flabbergasted about my decision not to know.

"We just want to be surprised, that's all," I shrugged.

I felt my belly tense up suddenly, and I placed a hand on my belly as I looked out to the water. I took a couple of short breaths waiting for the sharp pain to pass. As the sun began to set, it cast a warm golden glow across the vast expanse of the ocean. The gentle waves crashing against the hull of the ship was a sight to behold.

"You really shouldn't be out here on the ocean," said Keera as she watched me. "You're out here having contractions."

"It's not the real contractions," I said, gulping with fear that she could be right. As an ex-nurse, this was the dumbest mistake I could make. We were out in the middle of the ocean, but the chances of me having a baby within a three-hour span was unlikely.

But also possible.

"Ladies," said Vanessa, my sister-in-law, strolling up to us with a drink in her hand. We hugged, and Vanessa was careful not to squish my belly. "You're so big!"

My brother Jack and his pack were socializing with my alpha pack. It made my heart warm to see that.

"Thanks," I said sarcastically, and she laughed. "How's my brother treating you?"

"He's wonderful," said Vanessa dreamily, sipping her drink. "He makes sure I'm not being pushed around by the Royal Pack whenever I visit them for my son, Gabe."

"How about Alex, is he less of an ass?" I asked.

"I love Alex," she said in a low voice. "Don't let him hear that. We got into an argument this morning."

"Oh gosh," I said, shaking my head.

"Jade," said Caleb from behind me.

"Yes?" I asked, turning around.

He cleared his throat and looked around at everyone. I was confused. Dravin, Nick, and Bruce stood around him, looking at me with love in their eyes.

*What was going on?*

"My dearest Jade," Caleb's voice was rough but filled with love. My heart began thumping in my chest. "From the moment I met you, you've become a light in my heart. A light of hope, laughter, and love. I couldn't imagine spending my life with an omega who isn't you."

He took a step closer, and his kiss on my hand sent a warmth radiating down my body. He went down on one knee.

"Oh my god," I whispered, my hand to my mouth. I couldn't have imagined that he would propose today like this.

He reached into his pocket, retrieving a small velvet box. Then one by one, the rest of his pack went down on their knees, each presenting a single rose.

My heart was literally about to explode.

"From the moment I laid eyes on you at the Ball, I knew you were mine," said Bruce, grasping my hand. "Even though our pack leader was an ass at times, I fought through it to be with you and to love you."

I giggled through my tears while Caleb grunted.

"I know," I whispered.

"Will you marry me, Jade?" he asked.

"Yes," I said, taking the rose he handed me.

Dravin was next down the line. "You ignited a fire in my soul. You've brought the light and love back into our lives. Into *my* life. I love you. Will you marry me, Jade?"

"Yes, of course," I said, my hands shaking as I took the rose from him.

Lastly, Nick gazed at me with a tinge of pink on his face.

"Through the short time we spent together, you've made me comfortable to be around you," said Nick, his voice holding a tremor from his nervousness. I smiled encouragingly. "You make me feel like a true alpha and I want to spend the rest of my life with you. Will you marry me?"

"Yes," I answered, blushing as I took the rose from him as well.

"Will you allow us the honor of cherishing you, protecting you, and showering you with a love that knows no bounds?" said Caleb at last, opening the box displaying a ring with a brilliant diamond at its center, sparkling like a star in the sunset while smaller diamonds shimmered alongside it.

"Yes," I said, my voice trembling with emotion. My heart swelled with a mix of emotions as tears shimmered in my eyes. I looked into the eyes of each alpha, feeling their love envelop me. "Caleb, Bruce, Dravin, Nick - I would love nothing more than to marry you. A thousand times, yes!"

Caleb's hand trembled as he pulled the ring from the box. His gaze locked on mine as he slowly slid the ring onto my finger. His touch was tender yet possessive as he sealed his love for me.

One by one, the alphas rose, encircling me in their arms, creating an unbreakable bond I would never forget.

The night sky seemed to burst with joy as everyone, who had been silently witnessing this magical moment, erupted into applause and cheers, their voices harmonizing with the rhythm of the sea.

I gasped suddenly as another contraction seized me. I leaned against Dravin as the other alphas still surrounded me from the hug. My thighs dripped with liquid.

"Oh no," I groaned.

"Is it the baby?" asked Bruce.

"My water just broke," I said, gasping for air when the longest contraction of the night released me.

"Fuck," said Caleb.

As another contraction gripped me a second apart, I knew I was in trouble. I was feeling pressure between my legs. I screamed from the pain, and chaos erupted on the yacht. I couldn't stand up straight anymore as Dravin held onto me.

"Are we near land?" Nick shouted to the captain. "She's about to give birth!"

"No sir," the captain responded. "It will be at least another hour."

With each contraction, the pain intensified, gripping me with a vice-like grip that seemed to squeeze my body from the inside out. It felt like my muscles were being stretched beyond their limits, demanding every ounce of my strength and endurance. The waves of agony seemed never-ending, crashing against my body with unrelenting force.

Dravin laid me down, and I twisted onto my side, trying to find a comfortable position. Anything to help the pain as he urgently purred into me, and Nick purred onto my other side. They were trying to create a wave of peace in a storm of pain raging through me.

And there was no fucking medicine on here to numb it.

"Give her air!" shouted Keera, rushing to me.

I clenched my teeth, fighting back the urge to scream, afraid that the sound would somehow amplify the pain.

"What do you need, Keera?" Caleb asked as she positioned me with my knees up.

"A shoelace and blankets," she said urgently. "Hot water if possible. Jade, what's the pain from 1-10?"

"9," I groaned. My breaths came in short, rapid gasps as I desperately tried to find any semblance of relief.

"Help me lift her dress out of the way," Keera said, and Bruce quickly lifted my dress over my thighs. Even through my pain, I didn't want the whole ship watching me. Keera saw that in my eyes. "Let's move her below deck. Now! Before the baby crowns."

Everything was a blur as Nick and Dravin carefully held me in their arms, rushing down the steps of the ship. I felt nauseous and seasick from the wobbly ship on top of the pain from my contractions.

*Please god, let this be over with quickly*, I prayed.

This was my worst-case scenario, and I hoped I would make it out alive.

I was lying on a bed and screamed when another contraction squeezed me. Someone had removed my dress and underwear.

Keera peered between my legs. And her face turned white.

"What is it, Keera? Tell me!"

"The baby's breech," she said calmly. "Don't panic, Jade. We've birthed a million babies for omegas before. Trust every word I tell you to do, okay?"

"What in the hell?!" exclaimed Caleb.

"My wife knows what she's doing," said Jatix loudly from across the room. "Just listen to her."

A tremor of sheer panic rolled over me.

"Oh my god," I cried out as I felt the pain swelling again. More persistent. More urgent.

"Don't push," said Keera, placing her hand on my round belly her fingers tracing the baby's position. "I have to push the baby's feet back in."

I gritted my teeth and gripped my alphas' hands as she moved me in different positions, trying to manually adjust the baby's position. With every move, it felt like fire piercing down my belly to my privates.

"Argh!" I shouted.

"Jade, listen carefully," said Keera, looking at me eye to eye. An unspeakable bond of trust formed between us, and feminine energy radiated in the room. "I want you to push now. I can see the baby's head now."

Taking a deep breath, I pushed with all my might, screaming as the pain intensified. The atmosphere was charged with anticipation as Keera's skilled hands glided all around my belly, constantly manipulating the baby's position.

"Again," she ordered.

"I'm so scared," I whimpered.

"You are strong," said Caleb.

Caleb kissed my forehead, and I closed my eyes, pushing again, allowing the pain to sear through me.

"Push baby," said Dravin. "Squeeze my hand as tight as you want."

I clung to Keera's steady presence, drawing strength from the fact that she would lead me to a successful birth. Time seemed suspended, minutes stretching into eternity as I pushed and pushed.

Keera's hands skillfully guided the baby out, and I cried out when the pain stopped.

A fragile cry filled the air, and everyone in the room cheered as Keera held the baby in her arms.

"It's a girl," she said, smiling at me.

"Oh goodness," I sighed, smiling weakly. I was so happy it was a girl. I would dress us up in matching cute outfits.

I reclined against the pillows. My body drenched in exhaustion. I took deep breaths as Nick fanned me with a cardboard, and Caleb kissed me all over my face in relief from this dangerous birth.

My four alphas gazed upon our newborn girl in a cocoon of tenderness and awe. After Keera wiped the baby down, she carefully placed the baby against my chest, skin-to-skin. The alphas approached my side, forming a formidable shield against the world.

It was our moment.

Dravin gently brushed a strand of damp hair away from my brow, his touch feather-light. My heart swelled with love for my newborn and for my alphas who encircled me protectively.

I looked at Keera and smiled. A true friend through thick and thin.

"Thank you, Keera," I said. "I owe you one."

"And I'll remember it too," she said jokingly. "Congratulations, sister."

"God, she's so beautiful," I said, gazing down at my baby's tiny little face. So fragile and so perfect.

"She really is," muttered Bruce.

"Her name will be Olivia," I whispered.

"It's perfect," said Caleb, gently kissing the baby's hand. "It's official then. Our daughter Olivia Moonworth born to the Moonworth Pack, will be protected and cared for until we draw our last breath."

Each alpha leaned in, pressing a gentle kiss against my forehead, sealing their vow to cherish and protect our precious child and me. And as I held our baby in my arms, surrounded by the unwavering love of my four alphas, I knew that our journey was meant to lead us to this very moment.

**THE END**

Bonus scene! Read on for the wedding day scene, which ends with a steamy wedding night: Matched to The Pack: Bonus Scene

URL for Bonus Scene: https://BookHip.com/BNTQJPQ

Continue on to **Book 6,** Knotted by The Pack – This story will follow Tiana's daughter (Alana) on her journey to find true love with her pack and an unexpected pregnancy. If you haven't read Tiana's story yet, read Book 1 (***Stolen by The Pack***).

# Author's Note

**Thank you so much for reading!**

Thank you so much for reading *Matched to The Pack*. I hope you enjoyed reading this one, because I especially had fun writing it.

If you've made it this far, I'd appreciate it so much if you left a review on Amazon, letting me know what you think! It helps authors like me keep building stories for you to enjoy for a long time to come.

Please let me know what you'd like to see more from me and the hottest scenes you like from the book that I can expand on the next. This book was born from reader feedback and what they've liked the most from past stories. You can include your feedback in the review or you can email: author_laylasparks@yahoo.com.

Farewells...until the next story! <3

# Also By Layla Sparks

**Howl's Edge Island: Omega For The Pack Series (Reverse Harem Series)**

**Book 1 (Tiana's story):** Stolen by The Pack

**Book 2 (Keera's story):** Auctioned to the Pack

**Book 3 (Lyra's story)**: Princess For The Pack

**Book 4 (Vanessa's story)**: Betrayed by The Pack

**Book 5 (Jade's story)**: Matched to The Pack

**Book 6 (Alana's story)**: Knot for The Pack

**Captive After Moonlight Series: DARK Romance (short novella)**

Jenna gets a lot more than she can handle when visiting the smutty toy shop downtown. She looks for the perfect naughty toy, but little does she know that a werewolf is looking for *his* toy...

Now she's kidnapped by a psycho HOT werewolf who believes Jenna should be his.

**Book 1**: Werewolf's Mate

**Book 2:** Werewolf's Captive

**Five Sexy Bigfoot Short Stories: Kink For Monsters**

**Book:** Five Sexy Bigfoot Short Stories

**Alien Erotica Series: Tantalizing Tentacles of Korynz: (Kidnapping & Age Gap/ Short Stories)**

**Book 1**: Disciplined by My Alien Teacher

**Book 2**: Examined by My Alien Doctor

**Book 3**: Enslaved by The Alien King

-On Kindle Unlimited

Printed in Great Britain
by Amazon

29858740R00130